Poke Sallet Queen
and
the Family Medicine Wheel

A Novel

Shana Thornton

Thorncraft Publishing
Clarksville, Tennessee

First Edition, 2015

Published in the United States by Thorncraft Publishing. No part of this book may be reproduced, by any means, without written permission from the author and/or Thorncraft Publishing. Requests for permission to reproduce material from this work should be sent to Thorncraft Publishing, P.O. Box 31121, Clarksville, TN 37040.

This book is made possible by the love and support of Nancy Morris.

This novel is a work of fiction. Names, characters, incidences, and places are the products of the author's imagination or used fictitiously. Any resemblance to actual individual people, living or dead, places, or events is completely coincidental.

ISBN-13: 978-0-9857947-5-0
ISBN-10: 0985794755

Cover Design by etcetera...
Poke Sallet drawing on title pages by Shana Thornton.
Author photograph by Terry Morris.
No part of this book cover may be reproduced, by any means, without written permission from Thorncraft Publishing.

Library of Congress Control Number: 2015901106

Thorncraft Publishing
P.O. Box 31121
Clarksville, TN 37040
http://www.thorncraftpublishing.com
thorncraftpublishing@gmail.com

Printed and Bound in the United States of America

10 9 8 7 6 5 4 3 2 1

For Mom & Dad

ACKNOWLEDGMENTS

This book has been growing a long time—a lifetime, and first, I thank my parents who encouraged my interests and bought book after book for me. My Mom has read stories and drafts and given valuable feedback and support, while my Dad provided advice on recipes, wildlife, and so much more. Your garden and love of plants informed the book more than you will ever know. Thank you for embracing my life and challenging me to reach for my goals and dreams.

Holding my hand and, sometimes, dragging me forward with the reminder that I am strong and all that I create is for a higher purpose—to give something back to others and create a business that is an example to my daughters about the importance of following your heart and talents, while honoring women's literature and the stories by and about women. Terry, you are my hero for encouraging that message and uplifting all of the authors and people who work with Thorncraft. Your business guidance prompted a beginning and has continued to help us grow. Families are the inspiration behind this book, and my daughters, Zoe and Silvia, set forth the true blooming of my life, and I am thankful for their acceptance of my need for solitude and writing time, but more for their disruptions that provoke laughter and joy and free my heart to write with more presence and less demand.

Many women in my family never failed to hook me with a great story and listened to me when I spoke, even as a child. Jean Thornton Dennis, you fed me while I sat at your counter, and I talked until you made me go to bed at night. I was shaped by the beautiful gardens surrounding your house, and how hard you worked to make your life beautiful. When I see you, I am proud of your strength and knowing that you shaped me. I like your sense of humor, and watching *The Carol Burnett Show* and *Mama's Family* with you helped form my sense of family humor. The stories about your childhood, and all of the drawers of photographs you let me prowl through, helped me to see and understand the changes in our family and part of the world.

I'm grateful to Linda and Willard Mayberry for helping with my research for this book. Aunt Linda, your books and maps, photocopies and stories were pivotal. We enjoyed talking about the past with you and visiting the places where our family roamed. We love bringing the girls and spending time with you—that's the best research to me.

Storytelling is about presence, after all, and the women in my family who held family tales, old gossip, and theories in high esteem have shaped this book the most. My two aunts, oh how you were like sisters to me. Nancy Ferguson, you have commanded a captive audience throughout my life, and when you speak about the past, you are instilled with the authority of our ancestors. Your belief in the power of story is contagious, and I'm so glad you gave it to me. I admire your appetite for stories and living life to the fullest. Julie Vaughn, you listened and sang and danced, and that offered me opportunity to play and learn. Thank you for sharing a love of poetry, for switching poems with me, for exploring our spiritual feelings through words, and giving me many of my favorite books. My dear aunts, you both looked through countless photo albums and gave me the faces to match many stories.

I wouldn't know as much about many topics without conversations with Bill Ferguson, but for this book, I'm glad that you shared your knowledge of long rifles, the Civil War, Native American trade practices, and whatever topics mentioned herein that I'm forgetting.

My soul sister, Rita Yerrington, has been the editor for character development in this book and read every version a few times. You've given me the gift of true friendship and you are my family, and my life needed those two to merge in this beautiful way. Thank you for shoveling manure with me, planting flowers, for taking the time to not only smell the roses but to talk to them, and for encouraging lovely blooms. Thank you for your culinary insights and for making delicious meals over the years.

Kitty Madden and Beverly Fisher—your editing skills and advice propel me forward and lift me up at the same time. Kitty, I'm grateful for the time and care you take with every book. So much of my journey has been bolstered by your confidence and enthusiasm. I love you both and thank you always.

Barry Kitterman—thank you for your writing advice from "Intro to Creative Writing", to grad school classes, to post-publishing support and guidance. I wrote the first drafts of some parts of this novel in your creative writing courses, and they offered an environment for growth and creativity. When you submitted an early draft of chapter one to the Languages and Lit department for their annual Dogwood Award in Creative Writing, that signal of confidence helped me at a critical time.

Deb Burdin, thanks for reading the first chapter years ago and asking some tough questions about the characters. Thank you for our conversations and your feedback about the finished novel.

I needed demonstrations for part of this book, and Matt Ferguson, thank you for providing me with them.

Thank you to Terri Jordan, Ellen Kanervo, Amy Wright, and Peggy Bonnington for giving me opportunities to share my work with an audience in Clarksville.

Candice Read Shoulders, thank you for creating beautiful photographs that inspired me while I wrote this book.

The first chapter was published as an earlier version in *The Round Table*, Volume XLIII. Thank you to Editor Brett Ralph, and to Kelly Moffett, the guest judge, for choosing it as the winner of the Robert Penn Warren Award.

My Ma, Audra Brown, though she's not with us anymore, she gave so much of her life to this book—encouraging me to write letters to her and to write stories and newspaper articles. She was the first person I interviewed in my life, at fourteen-years-old, and as the years passed, I asked her so many questions about her life that she was annoyed with me. To all of those who have passed on to the other side, I humbly bow and give thanks for your presence in my life—for sharing stories with me: Nancy Morris and her support of this way of life for me, Granddaddy Charles Thornton and his love of radio broadcasts, Great Mommy Hattie Thornton and her preservation of the old timey way of life, Pa Junior Brown and his willingness to share the ways of the barnyard, Aunt Lyda Adams and her big cackling laugh like the peacocks she raised, Aunt Nanney Brown and her intricate house, Uncle B Ballard and his uncanny zest for shenanigans and storytelling, Thurla Lee Lindboe and her adoration of birds and plants, and Gammy Nancy Vaughan and her love of literature, music, family stories, and Nashville.

Poke Sallet Queen
&
the Family Medicine Wheel

"Poke Sallet (n.), or poke, pokeweed, pokeberry, is a wild plant, sending out flexible red stems in the spring with leafy greens, and growing swiftly to a gangly, bright height with a crown of nodding, toxic berries. It sends down a tap root that can reach some ten feet or more under the earth. The young, tender shoots are fried and the greens boiled in the spring for food reminiscent of turnips or spinach. Purple pokeberries, which are toxic if eaten especially in large quantities, have been used to make dyes and inks."—from a scrap of paper found in Hoot Ballard's journal (source unknown)

SHANA THORNTON

PROLOGUE

Robin Ballard, 2010

This is not a lonely story about somebody and their nobodies. My big, busybody family with their too-many talents demands an audience for understanding themselves. They weren't born knowing their own strengths, as some families are with parchment scrolls and crests that open doors, hands that have shaken deals generations ago—no, my family learned that the simple handshake isn't the parchment or signature, isn't a lineage. Our knowledge would come from the dirt.

I'm one of those people who have to practice over and over to get a talent. Development, that's what someone will do for mastery. We want it to come naturally and be easy, but too often, only the desire is natural and easy. The rest takes concentration, passion, and a kind of desperation that propels you forward. Those are Aunt Cora's words, and she's actually my great aunt. She told me about the talents—how everyone has the potential for at least one. Because she is over ninety years old, I believe it when she says that natural talent is rare—most people need time to develop a skill. "I didn't understand people, how they are, their little social quirks and all," she said. "Until I could size up a person based on their talent. Then every person became clear to me. The talent was like a map of their motives and intentions. It shows a person's ambition for the dream goal that's in their head—it'll push right through someone. Magnetizing and pulling them toward mastery and union with their talent."

Trying my hand at writing is the talent I'm going for. Being a "know-it-all," Aunt Cora laughed. I agreed that maybe writers are some type of know-it-all, collecting information to give it back to the people who can't go around and collect the tales from each individual in a family. One of my professors told us to do that in a creative writing class I was taking for an elective, and that's what got me here to the page, and the professor's instructions would become more than an assignment in an elective—taking over my identity, I set out on some sacred quest unknowingly. Let me be straight, I was way too distracted to understand the unfolding of a story. Walking into that college classroom, I was more interested in flirting than learning; though I would eventually be focused enough to overcome the odds my family stacked against me and surpass the hope they maintained for me, I was at a precarious turning point the fall of my sophomore year. The state scholarship I managed to secure was in jeopardy. Attending more parties than classes, I was spiraling toward family tradition—I wasn't scoring grades to make my family proud.

That writing class changed my focus. The professor brought in a video about five minutes long of her grandma telling a story about when the teacher was born. Some students seemed curious, others were bored, and I was simply happy to be watching a video instead of writing straightaway. While I wondered hopefully if she would play a lot of videos during the semester, she asked how many of us had heard the story of our birth from a parent or other relative. "Maybe you get bored with hearing about your family's stories, the ones they tell over and over. If not about when you were born, something else. Maybe they embarrass you when they tell stories to your boyfriends or girlfriends, to your friends, at inappropriate times. Believe me, if you haven't experienced this by now, you will at some point. Maybe you have a friend group who is your family. The same dynamic happens in the family unit, no matter the blood relations present. We need people and they need us. We use each other for everything, including the entertainment and wisdom found in storytelling, our basic family stories about how we came to be—whether that means how you came to be born and living together or if you live together through another circumstance. Regardless, we have bonding stories. My grandma, whom you just watched in the video, died last week. I made this video two months ago, along with a series of other interviews with her. I want you to think about someone in your family that you consider a storyteller and go get one of those stories."

Our first assignment was to tell a story from our family, and if we needed to interview someone to get started and use their voice, that was okay, as long as we told the story on paper in some way. Throughout the semester, we developed the storytelling of our families, those we could reach out to and find. Each assignment slanted our approach to the interview or retrieval of information, and my plan branched out to include finding lost journals and letters. For that initial assignment, I thought that I better talk to my Dad first because I didn't know if he would live too much longer. I've always thought he was tempting fate, and at the time of my writing class, he was homeless, living on the street somewhere outside of Nashville, and I decided to go track him down. But if I wanted to know exactly where he was living, I needed to talk to his mother, my grandma, Miss Emy. And yes, she was called that formal name by her own Mama, and known to everyone, including her grandchildren, as Miss Emy, and it was respected.

CHAPTER 1

ASSIGNMENT ONE

When I arrived at Miss Emy's house, she wasn't forthcoming about where my Dad might be—she was more interested in telling her story to me. She wanted me to understand how she didn't fit in with the Ballard family, even though she married in and tried to understand their peculiarities. She took my fingers in her thin, little hummingbird hands, and the fan was still clasped in our folded hands somewhere—Miss Emy always carried a fan that was usually so busy fluttering that her hands never seemed to rest. She led me straight out the oval glass door to the back porch, down the stairs, and we followed the path in the lawn underneath the wide red oak and silver maples until we reached the gate to the medicine wheel. The wrought iron was rusted and flaking with coats of black paint. When Miss Emy opened the gate, the latch creaked and rattled the rose hips encircling it, announcing our entrance to the garden. I ducked underneath bawdy, thorny limbs, some as thick as a small tree with thorns over an inch long, that Miss Emy wouldn't cut since they produced blush-colored single roses with a yellow center and a sweet cinnamon-style fragrance that drifted up off the fields and got carried away by the clouds during the springtime. That day during the autumn, they were dark and protective, and my shirt snagged on a thorn. The tree-lined paths merged and spiraled out again in little turns. Tucked away into mossy spots, wildflowers grew in a mysterious cold shade by the rock bench that sheltered more secret plants. They bloomed tiny flowers, strange cultivars that defy ordinary maintenance and thrive on wild abandon. There were sensible vegetables and legumes, the thorny and soft of the bark, fungi, and blooms. I knew the medicine wheel was an old planting, probably started by my great-great-grandmother Nenny, and that Miss Emy, my grandmother, maintained it, but the importance of its magical place in my life evaded my conscious awareness until the day I visited Miss Emy about my college assignment.

We sat down in the medicine wheel and I listened to her story, as she nervously fluttered her fan.

Miss Emy's Story, 1950-1968

When she first saw Zona Ballard, Miss Emy knew that Zona was a witch even though everyone in Granville said she was an Indian. She didn't remember who was having the baby the first time she stared at Zona, because she was only a little girl. But Miss Emy would never forget that Zona wore silver rings on the middle part of both her little fingers, and her black hair was coiled into a knot on her head. The flowers in her winding braid were bright at her arrival. When she left, the faded yellow flakes of petals were ashes floating in the air behind her.

The women of Granville comforted themselves with believing that Zona's mother was the child of a lost Shawnee or Chickasaw or a clever Cherokee who managed to remain behind when the Indians were forced into a walk out West by a president from our own state centuries ago, because she was dark as mud. Zona was the midwife in town and delivered all the babies alongside Dr. Davis. If the pregnant woman was accustomed to having babies, he didn't even attend the birth. He let Zona handle it by herself. She delivered her own twelve children, all boys except two, so she was an expert. Miss Emy's husband, Paul, was Zona's last child, and she just squatted over the chamber pot and birthed him in twenty minutes. At least, that's how she told the story when Miss Emy was pregnant for the first time and scared about the pain. Miss Emy maintains that she didn't trust Zona then, so Dr. Davis delivered Carolyn, Miss Emy and Paul's first daughter. It took seven hours. In the 1950s, Dr. Davis and Zona were still making house calls. Miss Emy forbade Paul to let Zona in the house. They were at odds with one another since Zona insisted on using her magic to ensure Miss Emy's baby was a boy, so Miss Emy had a girl just to spite her.

"Emy," Dr. Davis said, "you need to make peace with Zona. You're having her grandchild and living on the Ballard farm." He stood at the end of the bed. Miss Emy shivered in the December air that seemed to be pushing through the walls and windows. The sweat from her hair crawled across her scalp in tremors, and contractions seized her muscles and joints, digging through to her bones.

"Can't I just have my baby and enjoy it?" Miss Emy asked him. "Why do I always have to be the one to make peace? I didn't even want to live out here on their land." She tried to gaze out the window and forget about her stifled breathing. Dr. Davis's daughter, Hazel, was her best friend and she agreed to assist in the delivery. She had shared the whole pregnancy with Miss Emy, watching her belly swell and dreaming of tiny baby parts. She gave Miss Emy water and tried to make the peace. The ceiling light was on, and all Miss Emy could see was her own reflection in the glass, sulking back.

"Concentrate on your breathing," Hazel said. She turned to Dr. Davis. "Why don't you take a break and have a cup of coffee in the kitchen? I can monitor her progress."

"At least you've got people around who care for you," he said. He picked white knots of lint from his pants and twirled them between his fingernails. That episode was so reminiscent of Miss Emy's father, Judge Simpson (who everybody called Square Simpson), and the Judge and Dr. Davis had been the closest of friends. Dr. Davis knew this phrase would remind Miss Emy to feel guilty about her mother, and it seemed like everyone had always blamed Miss Emy for the tragedy. Miss Emy got so used to tragedy from the very beginning, that's what she was drawn to.

Miss Emy was so little, maybe four years old. She'd knocked over the candles that caught the drapes on fire. They told her that she had run around her Mama and into the hallway and up the stairs. That's what the cook, Mrs. Timms, said, that Miss Emy just dashed through the rooms until her Mama was lost in the smoke. Then, next thing she knew, Mrs. Timms found Miss Emy standing in the front yard, crying that she couldn't find her Mama. The house rolled dark clouds out of its roof; that's all Miss Emy could remember. Mrs. Timms had said that she didn't know what else to do except to look for Miss Emy's baby brother and the jewelry box. Her baby brother later died from smoke inhalation.

Some people in the town never passed up an opportunity to explain why Miss Emy should be grateful for the circumstances of her life, especially since her father was overheard lecturing about it so many times with his high moral superiority, and even on his death bed, suffering with tuberculosis.

When she was giving birth for the first time, Dr. Davis ordered her. "Just let Paul's family in the house," he said. "They're standing in the cold on the porch. Paul feels pulled between his parents and you."

Miss Emy was in pain with contractions. She felt like her groans sank into the floor around Hazel, who just stared at her. "They're too close, that's the problem," Miss Emy said. "I can't escape. For God's sake, they live on the next damn hill."

"You'll be moving when Paul finishes the house," Dr. Davis said and stopped twirling the lint during the pause. "Don't you think it's selfish not to share the birth of this child with your husband's family, with your mother-in-law?"

She was having major contractions and all he wanted to do was lecture. Moving to Nashville was taking a long time. Paul bought a house after he started working at the Ford glass plant, but it needed major repairs. Miss Emy waited in Granville through the week while Paul worked in Nashville. On the weekends, he came home to help his father with the farm. Being pregnant and alone with her in-laws annoyed Miss Emy. She was always thankful to have Hazel's sympathy when the pressure from the family overwhelmed her.

"Who's waiting on the porch?" Miss Emy asked Hazel.

Dr. Davis cleaned all the silver instruments on the dresser even though he never used more than two of them. "Hoot and Zona and the two sisters," he said quickly. Paul's father Hoot Ballard usually kept to himself. Miss Emy said that before that night, she never heard him say more than a few words at a time and those were about plants or animals on the farm. She couldn't believe that he had waited for the birth. He seemed more interested in talking to men and dealing with business than attending a birth.

Miss Emy buried her face in a pillow during the next contraction. Panting through a sudden, cold fog, she heard Hazel. "Emma, look at me and breathe or he'll put you under," she said. "And, I know you want to be awake for this like we've been talking about, so try to concentrate. We're ready to deliver your baby. I need you to push, Emma." Miss Emy's eyelids flickered open. "Breathe and push, breathe and push," Hazel said. She held Miss Emy's foot in her hands. "Think how you're becoming a mother like so many women throughout history," she said. Miss Emy gritted her teeth, lifting up from the bed. "Hush, Hazel!" she snapped and then screamed out and shook with sweat.

Dr. Davis looked as if he were delivering a pig or a mule, completely indifferent. He spoke to Hazel, but Miss Emy couldn't hear everything. "Too slow," is the only phrase she understood. She started to cry, but Hazel scolded her right back. "Now, you hush up, Emma! Listen to me and do this. Push, now!" Musical sounds thumped, plucked, and scratched through the air. Miss Emy didn't know where they were coming from, outside somewhere or her own self. The music seemed to grow louder as Miss Emy hurt more.

Hazel kept saying, "Breathe and push! Breathe and push!" She blocked the doctor with an arm. Dr. Davis muttered and walked to the table for scissors.

"What is that noise?" Miss Emy asked. "Hazel!" Miss Emy screamed. "I can't take much more. Dear God!" Miss Emy begged and stared up at the ceiling. She cried out. Hazel and Dr. Davis didn't seem to hear anything. Miss Emy thought the music was louder and more intense, and wasn't sure if her moans shook the bed or if the ground shuddered from the musical vibrations. She screamed.

"Is she hallucinating?" Hazel asked her father. "The pain might be too much. Maybe you should knock her out."

Miss Emy screamed and pushed over and over, as the music reached a frenetic tangle of instruments.

"Good," Dr. Davis said and put down the scissors. "Keep pushing like that and I won't have to cut you."

Inside, Miss Emy begged the baby to escape from her body quickly. The tension of her limbs shook with the fear of exposed loneliness. Memories jumped into her mind like sudden lightning. She hadn't thought about the time she was lost in the thunderstorm while walking home from Mrs. Timms's in the middle of the night. It never entered her mind until then, but left a part of remembrance back in the hollow where she couldn't see the old roads. The mud had clumped on the soles of her feet. Clay gathered to trip her up. Her lightning scream echoed with her fears, just as it had when she was seven and lost, no lights to guide the way, just a blind fumbling, reaching out for trees, caught up in barbed wire, a tangled mess that she ripped herself out of and through and toward the lights of her new house and the front porch, where she cried for comfort; but her father, Square Simpson, hadn't noticed.

Miss Emy was pushing the baby out at the same time that she was remembering how she felt when she was lost that time.

"There she is," Hazel said.

"Who?" Miss Emy glanced at the window. "What is the noise?"

"You've torn yourself," Dr. Davis said. "I'll have to clean you up and put in some stitches."

"Our baby girl," Hazel said. "Pay attention, Miss Emy."

"Help me with this," Dr. Davis said to Hazel.

Holding her baby, Carolyn, for the first time, Miss Emy longed to know how a mother's embrace would feel. Her tears salted the wrinkled baby, who scratched at Miss Emy's breast with puckered fingertips.

"How do you feel?" Dr. Davis asked.

"She's perfect and beautiful," Miss Emy said. "I should be tired, but I can't believe that…."

"Let me rephrase," he interrupted. "Do you want to remain in seclusion or would you like to invite your family inside to see their new baby?"

"I'll go tell Paul that mother and daughter are okay," Hazel said quickly and pursed her lips.

"Just let everyone inside," Miss Emy said.

****

Hoot Ballard turned out to be Miss Emy's hero. From the moment Hoot laid eyes on Carolyn, he fell in love. She was a stroke of luck for Miss Emy. I guess after Zona gave Hoot so many boys, he was ready to spoil a granddaughter. Of course, he had other grandchildren of both genders, but none of the other children lived on the farm. Most of Paul's brothers were factory workers or had farms of their own. Both of Paul's sisters had married and moved closer to Nashville.

Because Paul and Miss Emy were the only family left living on the farm, Hoot and Zona were constantly bringing leftovers or coming by to check on anything and everything.

Two years later, Miss Emy said *no* to Zona's magic again and gave birth to another girl, Melinda. Paul and Miss Emy still lived on the farm. Zona didn't come to their house very often, but Hoot visited daily.

At noon, his truck bounced over the mud holes in the road, which led from the tobacco fields. If it was nice outside, Miss Emy took their lunch to the picnic table in the yard. Hoot always ate peanut butter and strawberry jam. He fed small spoonfuls of both peanut butter and jam to the girls, too. As they aged, both of them had long, shiny, straight hair. They dangled their tan arms from curvy dresses. "Look just like the Ballards," everyone said. With the four of them eating lunch together, Miss Emy studied their features.

"My mother was a Shawnee," Hoot said after she asked about his family. "She cultivated all those rose bushes," he pointed. Their pink, red, and golden tinted buds glowed like delicate orbs through the summer, especially when it rained. The raindrops beat out hundreds of petals like confetti and flowery snowflakes that cascaded into the forest.

"You mean Nenny, your mother?" He nodded his head and smiled. Miss Emy was always curious about Zona, and she seized the moment to ask. "So, where is Zona's family?" Miss Emy asked.

"My parents are Colonel Ballard and Nenny. All of my children were born here and now yours, too." He looked proud, took a deep breath, and straightened his spine. "Zona's family's from Virginia," he said.

"But I've always heard Zona's family was Cherokee from Kentucky," Miss Emy said.

He shrugged. "Where'd you hear that tale?"

Miss Emy blushed. She couldn't remember. Hoot surveyed the land as if he were looking for a marker that might tell the story of how it all came to be with the families. "I like that rose more than the seven sisters." He pointed to a climbing bush on the corner of the old shed toward the back of the house. Tiny flower buds had begun to grow and were almost black from being so small, but the red tips hinted at their true color. "The color of those roses is the color of Melinda's hair," he said. "The mixture of dark and light. The red shines in the sun."

"Your mother cultivated that rose bush, too?" Miss Emy asked. He nodded his head that she had, and he continued gazing around the yard and over the trees and hills. Hoot's high cheekbones were cut precisely to match the short, auburn hair above his ears. He was handsome, of course, but with a sharp intensity like stout, good liquor that sits up tall, the same kind that he made in the hollows. And, that was Paul's similarity, a knack for making whiskey and money.

"Can the girls come to the house tonight?" Hoot asked Miss Emy, finally flashing his smile. His teeth pointed precisely, and watching his mouth smile and talk was captivating to Miss Emy, another match that Paul carried with him.

But, Miss Emy wasn't thinking about that at the time—it only comes in the retelling…. What she was really thinking about was that everyone who wanted to hide their past or the misdeeds of their family just said they were from Virginia. That state was a safe bet. It didn't have any of the rebellious or exotic mystery of farther Southern states like Louisiana, Mississippi, and Georgia. She was turning it all over in her mind when she told him "yes" and watched him lift the girls into the truck before realizing what she had agreed to.

It was a Monday. The Ballards lived by the moon and had a lot of odd practices and beliefs. They worked on Sundays, since those days were ruled by the sun and best for productivity. They rested and conjured on Mondays when the moon commands control. Miss Emy learned about it after she married into their family. That's how she came to be at odds with Zona in the first place. It all scared her in the beginning. She had never seen nor heard of people like the Ballard family. Of course, people in town excused them as "Indians" and later, "hippies or something like that."

Every Monday, the family gathered for a spiritual meeting, which she called ghost story time. It didn't sit right with Miss Emy to begin with because, unlike the Ballards, she went to church every Sunday. Paul attended Sunday service with her most of the time, so she went to his family's spiritual meetings. They gathered in the medicine wheel, "a big circular garden," as Miss Emy described it, that "supposedly has special plants and trees with healing powers." Just looked like what you find deep in the forests, to Miss Emy, but, she would often say, "some of the strangest feelings wash over me when I'm sitting in the circle, even if it's warm enough for the flowers to bloom and make the prettiest views—it still gives me chills sometimes."

During one of those Monday nights, Zona shuffled playing cards. Paul had two sisters, Cora and Jane. After Zona fanned the cards across the grass—a little patch that bloomed tiny white flowers and was cold and soft under the witch hazel tree—she told Jane to pick three. Jane said,

"I just want something to happen, Mama. I know that I shouldn't ask you to read the cards, but I really appreciate it."

"It's no bother," she said and stopped her daughter's hand while it reached for a card. "I'll use my special ones." Zona opened a little box and brought out wide, tall colorful picture cards. The oil lamps flickered in the dusk, and a high moon rose over them. Jane's big breasts heaved in her dress, as if they glowed under her big eyes and dark hair. She hesitated, her dainty hand pushing a black curl behind her ear. Zona sighed and looked toward the clouds passing over the moon, darkening the evening a little faster. The men drummed in a circle around the fire, and someone plucked the strings of a banjo in a low tremble. The children laughed in the distance, chasing after crickets and toads. After Jane picked her cards, Zona flipped them over and said, "In two weeks and three days, transcendence will happen in your life. A new beginning of the heart."

Miss Emy thought maybe her fortune had a good message. She wanted to ask Zona but couldn't get the nerve, so she kept quiet and listened to Zona and Jane's conversation.

The stories of the evening spun around images from the cards. The one with a blackbird carrying a wrinkled worm in its beak made her shiver, especially after Jane's only son died on the day Zona prophesied. Doctor said, "His heart just stopped." Jane didn't have any other children and her sister Cora couldn't have babies. Nobody

22

talked about it—the sisters' lack of children. It was a sore spot, even though Jane told Miss Emy at her son's funeral, "If Mama hadn't prepared me by consulting the cards, I wouldn't be able to go on living. Because of that, I just knew it was meant to be. The poor baby was called to a higher purpose." Jane looked like she was all dressed to go out to a picture show, wearing a plum colored dress and hat. She was fresh with rouge and lip color.

Miss Emy couldn't go to their spiritual meetings after that. Her daughters had never sat in the Ballard family medicine wheel illumined by oil lamps and candles and listened to the weekly *spirit sightings*. They had never seen the witchcraft cards. Miss Emy tried not to be afraid. There was no sense in being afraid if she just kept away.

Sometimes, she just felt lured, especially by the melodies. All of it was hooey to her except for the music. Even though she didn't participate in their stories, she and the girls sat outside in the dark of our yard and listened to the banjos, fiddles, drums, and rattles call over from the next hill. It was powerful when one instrument played in a lonely song. The sound climbed the sky until it reached out, grabbed the hands of those listening, and made them clap together. Miss Emy couldn't tell the difference between drums and hands sometimes since the hands became the drums. By that time, Miss Emy and the girls could usually smell the hog cooking in the pit the Ballard family had put it in on Sunday evenings. The scent of meat smoldering drifted to their noses even on the most still of nights. You could actually smell it all day, but Miss Emy only remembers it as the most tempting part of the whole night. In order to overcome it, she fried slices of ham and potatoes for the girls.

That first Monday when Hoot took the girls, Miss Emy wanted to retaliate and thought about accusing him of tricking her. She thought about walking into their little ceremony and calling them all fools and witches. But, to take the girls away would have meant breaking the only relationship that mattered with one of Paul's family members. The thought of further isolation terrified Miss Emy and she couldn't be rude to Hoot. She was afraid everyone would resent her even more. The girls would know their own grandparents, even if Miss Emy thought they were crazy.

After that, she decided to let the girls go every Monday night so she could spend her time with Hazel, who lived in a small house beside the Granville post office. Hazel wanted to learn how to sew, an activity that had allowed Miss Emy to fill her time waiting for an absent father and later for an absent husband. Miss Emy made almost all the clothes for the girls. Hazel was bored and frustrated, trying to get pregnant. She wanted to sew some new curtains and learn how to crochet. It took two months for her to get one set of curtains right and to make one doily that she crocheted crooked, but they had the time because Hazel's husband worked and lived with Paul in Nashville.

Hazel didn't go away to college, even though Dr. Davis wanted to send her to become a nurse. Instead, she messed around with Luke. He had been a quarterback in high school. His father was an electrician, so the talent just sparked naturally in Luke. Usually, Hazel was the favorite do-gooder girl, but she was pregnant before tossing her high school graduation cap. She and Luke married the very next day. They went to the Opryland Hotel for three nights, where the bathroom was as big as Hazel's house, or so she said. She said the Opry was divine, and Miss Emy was envious that "Hazel was able to make the scene." They both wanted so badly to get out of Nowheresville, their nickname for Granville, but they ended up being jacketed by two boys rooted in the town.

Then, Hazel suffered a miscarriage. Just like that, suddenly, in the bath. And, Dr. Davis had no explanation. She was gone in her mind for a few months. That's when Paul and Miss Emy married and their pregnancy took hold. Hazel latched onto Miss Emy's pregnancy and started to plan the delivery. Hazel had been reading about different birthing methods, so she asked her father to keep Miss Emy awake. Before that, Miss Emy was so worried about Hazel, thinking she'd stay in a depression and never revive. A gray ash covered her usually white-rose body. Her delicacy had turned brittle, and Luke always seemed to be in a hurry, rushing with his head put down, so it was like an act of the divine when Paul landed the job at the glass plant and helped Luke get one, too.

Their house in Nashville needed major repairs, and had to be gutted because it was so old and out of date, and Paul decided to build onto it. Luke was helping with the electrical wiring while looking for a place where he could move Hazel. The four of them were fueled by that plan—

all living in Nashville. But it took longer than they'd expected since Paul only worked on the house after his regular job during the week. For a while, he appeased Miss Emy's desire for movement by buying her a new Thunderbird with his discount from the glass plant. That car just made her even more determined to move.

She and Hazel sometimes spent the weekend with their husbands, leaving the girls with their grandparents. One Saturday night while they played Hearts, Hazel shot the moon.

"Luke and I have decided to move to Detroit," she said after placing the Black Maria at the head of her row of hearts. Her fake eyelashes fluttered toward Luke while she lowered her head and giggled.

"What are you talking about, Hazel?" Miss Emy asked. She looked at Luke and Paul for an explanation when Hazel wouldn't answer. Hazel focused on picking at her fingernails while Miss Emy glared. She was good at glaring a long time at someone, waiting for the answer to burn straight up from a person's conscience and into their tongue and catch it on fire until they did the right kind of telling.

"Any of us at the plant here can transfer to a job at the assembly plant in Detroit if we want to," Luke said, folding his cards together. "The money's better and Hazel's sick of living by herself in Nowheresville." Hazel poked her lower lip into a red pout.

"But I'm there! What about me? And when are you moving?" Miss Emy asked. She tossed her remaining cards down on the center of the table for emphasis.

"We're going back to Granville tomorrow to pack up the house. We'll stay with Dr. Davis for a night or two," Luke said. "He's going to manage the house. We're renting it out."

"Why didn't you tell me about this?" Miss Emy asked Hazel. "I can't believe it. You conspired to leave Nowheresville and didn't tell me!"

"It's been a hell of a year, Miss Emy. You know that. She can't stay there thinking about...." He stopped short of saying her brother's name, but they all knew what he was getting at. Hazel's older brother, Milton (most people called him Milt, for short), had just vanished into thin air, and no one had heard from him. He came home from medical school, smart-alecky as usual, and bragging that he was about to become a doctor. Truth be told, it made Hazel furious to hear him boast all the time while she was in Granville helping her Daddy with patients. Then, that was it, he was just gone one day and never showed up at college, never heard from again. It had been just over a year. The whole town looked for him, and Dr. Davis paid a private investigator, and they all talked to him; it seemed he talked to just about everybody in town and up North at his college, but still, they never found Milt. They searched for him and his car. Miss Emy couldn't blame Hazel, but she was shocked that her best friend hadn't told her the truth about moving.

"Plus, it gives Dr. Davis something to manage, and he's planning to spend part of the year up North with us," Luke said and snapped his fingers at Miss Emy to pick up one of her cards that had fallen onto the floor when she'd become angry, so that he could reshuffle for a new game. "You can't blame Hazel for not telling you. No offense, Emma, but she knew you'd try to change her mind."

Miss Emy was frosted, a word she kept saying decades after it went out of popularity. She decided to devise her own plan of escape, and Hazel fueled her fire.

The other iron went in Miss Emy's fire when she got home at the end of that long weekend, and the girls came back telling all kinds of wild stories about spirits. They picked tomatoes out of the little garden in a field behind the house.

"How was your weekend?" Miss Emy asked. "Were you good girls and did you help Pa Hoot and Ma Zona?"

"Yes, we danced around a big fire," Melinda said. She twirled through the rows of sticky plants, squashing some of the fallen fruits under her heels. "It's the first of summer and the sun is the brightest."

"That sounds all right," Miss Emy said, filling the baskets. "Were there a lot of people playing drums and music?"

"Yeah, the drums were shaking the earth under us," she said trembling. Carolyn giggled and followed behind her, imitating her reenactment. She listed the names of all the people who were there, just Paul's siblings and their families. "And Ma Zona made a hot soup and sang after everyone ate it all," Melinda said and both she and Carolyn suddenly belted vowel sounds toward the sun. Miss Emy didn't understand the song, had never heard it. They tried to blow out from their bellies in order to make deep-sounding notes. Then suddenly, they screamed a squealing high note. The nearby birds scattered. They startled the big-eyed cows in a neighboring field.

Melinda continued without missing a breath. She was the informant, while Carolyn mothered her and laughed at her antics. Melinda investigated, talked, and coaxed Carolyn into following her on more adventures. "Ma Zona told us all about how she befriends spirits and they live with us here," Melinda said as they walked back to the house with baskets of peppers, tomatoes, leftover peas that survived in spite of the heat, a few early melons, clippings of dill, and tops of basil plants. "Ma Zona says they're our guides and they help to protect us. Some of them came from a lost tribe. But Ma Zona doesn't talk about them much since she didn't know them. Grandma Nenny tells the stories to keep them alive. Maybe even some gold coins buried by them." Melinda savored details. They both made spooky noises and giggled.

"There isn't any such thing as ghosts," Miss Emy said sternly. "That's just a bunch of silly nonsense! I don't want to hear you talk about it again. You tell Ma Zona that I said to stop telling stories."

After that weekend, Carolyn started having nightmares and sleepwalking. She had often been a fretful sleeper anyway, but this was different for Miss Emy to see her little daughter talk to invisible people and then scream. She fought and kicked something away from her bed, but she wasn't conscious. She had crossed over into some dream world that Miss Emy didn't like at all. Miss Emy caught her several times talking wide-eyed to an empty chair or the corner of a wall, so she decided to let Carolyn sleep in her bed whenever Paul was in Nashville through the week.

When Melinda cried to be in bed with them, too, Miss Emy began to feel smothered by her life. Even though they were all together with Carolyn in the middle, Miss Emy would wake up in the early morning hours and find that Carolyn wasn't in bed anymore. Miss Emy found her whispering in a low hum from the kitchen, and many times, Miss Emy was suddenly awakened by Carolyn's laughter echoing from another room in the house.

Carolyn stood beside the bed in the middle of the night and shook Miss Emy awake, saying, "Shhhh. A man is in the house."

Miss Emy jumped out of bed. "Where?" she asked.

"Through the hallway." But there was no one.

Each time the girls visited their grandparents, Miss Emy's home became a stranger to her. They'd crafted hanging symbols of yarn and sticks, even deerskin and feathers. Dangling from the light fixtures, on the windows, and tacked to a few trees, those webs scared Miss Emy. More than arts and crafts, she sensed what she thought were Zona's superstitions. When Miss Emy remembered Jane in her plum-colored dress, and the sadness of Cora's face when she seemed to remember that she couldn't have children, Miss Emy was angry but she wasn't sure why. She chastised herself, believing that she shouldn't have allowed the girls to get close to the Ballard family. She fought with herself for believing in witchcraft. She waved hands at herself, batted her imagination away, and tried to come up with the resolution about the girls' time with their grandparents.

Finally, when Paul came home one weekend and Miss Emy couldn't sleep alone with him, she stopped allowing the girls to attend ghost story time. Then, Miss Emy pressed Paul to stand by his word and move their family to Nashville. Six years was long enough to wait.

"I can't stand being away from all of you either. I hired two guys to finish what Luke and I didn't get to before he moved," Paul said. He stood in front of the percolator, waiting for it to heat up the coffee. "I plan on moving you next month. I've just got to finish painting and put up those two doors."

"When are you going to tell Zona and Hoot?" Miss Emy asked.

"I thought you'd be happy or even excited, not worried about my parents," he said. He tapped a spoon on the edge of his empty coffee mug. His fingers were callused and dark. "I've already told them. They've known about it for a couple weeks now. I thought the three of you might have talked about it."

"Why didn't you tell me first? Your family is so secretive. Paul, I didn't even know your grandmother was telling stories about a lost tribe and buried gold, until Melinda started telling their ghost stories," Miss Emy said. "Come on, your parents aren't offering up any more information than, *you might want to check out the blackberries over on the southern side, they've ripened nicely*. Or they knock in the morning, leave me milk, and say, *Morning. It's supposed to rain* or be *a pretty day* or whatever. What am I supposed to do?"

"You could have made more conversation yourself," Paul said. His eyes stared tensely from underneath the shadows of his hair. "They've always tried to do their best even if it doesn't always seem right, and they know you don't agree with their ways and I guess that makes them nervous."

"I don't understand their ways," Miss Emy said. "What are those things hanging everywhere? They're like giant spider webs. Everywhere! How can Zona make such scary things with kids?"

"Dream-catchers," he said. "Emma, calm down." He was laughing. "They're harmless, meant to give you good dreams from the spirit world, the earth. The spirit animals. Dad makes them, too."

"Hoot? I don't believe that. He seems more sensible. Go ahead, Paul, laugh if you want, but Carolyn has terrible dreams, and Melinda is telling these wild stories over and over. They're digging holes, looking for gold. All this nonsense or voodoo or whatever it is doesn't help!" Miss

Emy shouted. "This is crazy! How can an animal give me dreams?"

"It's not voodoo, Emma," he said. "I told you that you don't understand and if you would listen..." Miss Emy just stomped out. His voice called after her, "Maybe if you stopped for long enough to listen and talk, you'd know what they believe!"

The girls peeked from the corner. Miss Emy didn't want to fight when Paul came home on the weekend. She stormed down the slope of the yard to where it met the woods. The blackbirds that pecked under a small tree flew into the poplars, startling her. She walked the path toward Hoot and Zona's, the old Sears and Roebuck house, and it shone in white gabled glory on the hilltop. She could see a point of the roof here and there, and the white wood showing through the green leaves of the trees as she neared the porch. Hoot and Zona sat on the porch, but she continued on the trail around back and made her way to the medicine wheel. She sat in the center on the flat stone. She just sat there and smoked a cigarette, a defiant thrill she didn't often allow herself to have, letting it all go and feeling good that they were moving and that she was going to make it go by faster than a month.

****

Two weeks later, they were out of Granville and living in Nashville. Carolyn's nightmares worsened at first. Miss Emy put chairs in front of the doors so she wouldn't sleepwalk into the street. Their neighbor, Mrs. Clark, once led Carolyn home at 2 a.m. after hearing a repeated, banging noise. Carolyn had been swinging the gate back and forth, allowing it to hit against the post. "She had a far-off look," Mrs. Clark said, "so I knew she must've been sleepwalking like you told me about."

Paul worked third shift, so that left Miss Emy to deal with the same sleeping problems alone, and she still had to share her bed with Carolyn and Melinda for a while. After school, she often caught Carolyn and Melinda telling the ghost stories in a corner of the yard or house. Melinda wasn't good at whispering. Mrs. Clark always had her face pressed against the window when the girls were outside. She undoubtedly had the cleanest windows on the street. Miss Emy suspected that the girls were carrying on the Ballard family tradition and weaving ghost stories while sewing those hanging dream webs during their playtime. She tried to move the webby catchers away from Mrs. Clark's view, but the girls spun them faster than Miss Emy cared to collect them. Even though she was afraid of them becoming a spectacle around the neighborhood, or at least in Mrs. Clark's world, Miss Emy tried not to make a big deal out of their ghost stories and web catchers. That only made them focus more on Zona's magic, but eventually they almost convinced Miss Emy to become a believer of their ghosts during one night.

The three of them lay in bed, drifting toward sleep, and almost there. Miss Emy kept the light in the kitchen turned on so she could see if Carolyn, more than likely, wandered with her spirits. Carolyn couldn't turn the light out because it was in the center of the ceiling and had a short pull chain. The living room was between the bedroom and the kitchen. The light reflected across the hardwood floors in stretching and receding squares and triangles. Suddenly, the light went out. They were encompassed by darkness. But that helped with Miss Emy's drifting off to sleep, so she didn't mind the loss of light and reasoned the bulb had blown. Just as she was hoping the girls were completely asleep and hadn't noticed, in an echoing click, the light came back on. Then, back off again. On again, off. Just like that. The hair stood up on her arms. The girls were silent but stared out and pressed against her.

"I told you about them," Melinda tried to whisper. "It's ghosts for sure. Ma Zona told me this place has the most spirits." She started to cry.

"Stop it. Don't scare your sister," Miss Emy said.

"I'm not scared," Carolyn said.

"And what's that's supposed to mean anyway, *this place has more spirits*?" The constant flickering traced neon threads behind her eyelids.

"Ma Zona said that it's a bigger place and bigger places have more spooks," Melinda said. The electric energy was present but invisible except for the light that went on and off every thirty seconds. Miss Emy wondered why the light didn't blow for certain with all that motion. It started to rattle her cage and, ghost or not, Miss Emy threw the covers aside and walked quietly across the floors and into the kitchen.

Click, the light went off and she stood in the doorway trembling. Even though the streetlight was usually bright through the kitchen window, she couldn't see anything for the red and yellow streaks tracing through her vision. When it came on again, there was no one in the room except Miss Emy. There was nowhere to hide that quickly. She trembled, considered running, but waited; whether she would see a ghost or not, she decided to wait there and face it. If they were right, she resolved to see it. Nothing again. She stared up at the light bulb; her eyes watered. Then, she jumped back a little when she saw it, but caught herself, laughing silently at the tiny hand-like paw that she saw reach through a crack in the ceiling and pull the string of the light. Miss Emy felt satisfied with herself and her knowledge, her skepticism of superstitious beliefs. She walked back into the bedroom.

"Girls," she whispered, "you have to see this. Come on, I promise there's nothing to hurt you. It's an animal."

Melinda started to whimper and clung to Carolyn, who said, "Mama, you're scaring Melinda."

"A little animal," Miss Emy said quickly, "and it's in the attic. It can't get you."

The light still clicked a few times as they walked, holding hands, across the living room and into the kitchen doorway. Again, it went dark when they got there. Seconds later, the light came on. Miss Emy pointed for them to watch the light; the little paw dropped from the crack and both of them squealed and ran back to the bedroom. Miss Emy grabbed the broom from the corner and knocked its handle on the ceiling around the light. It stayed on for the remainder of the night.

Paul immediately reasoned it was a rat from their description. Miss Emy argued for a raccoon. He said a raccoon wouldn't care about the light anyway because they are nocturnal. Miss Emy thought rats were nocturnal, too. Paul said that a squirrel wasn't smart enough to click the light on and off, could a family be nesting in the attic, and that rats were definitely curious and weird enough to try something like that. He went up there to find out.

"Nothing," his voice echoed into the attic. He looked down at Miss Emy. "Just some dead bugs. It's dusty, that's for sure. There's no way a raccoon could have gotten in through this little window. Wait." He disappeared into the attic again.

"What kind of bugs?" Miss Emy called up into the dark space of the attic.

His face emerged in a small stream of light. "Moths and wasps. A couple of flies. There are some droppings," he said and dropped his hand down the ladder and leaned out. "Bring me some peanut butter to put on this trap. It's a rat."

Miss Emy didn't care. Rat or raccoon, she was just happy that it was an animal. She turned to the girls. "See there," she said. "No spirits in our attic. There's a reasonable explanation for most things."

She didn't move. "Can't you just put out poison?" Miss Emy asked Paul who ignored her question and descended the ladder.

"Animals are spirit messengers," Melinda said. "That's what Ma Zona says."

Carolyn chimed in, "Oh, yeah, spirit messengers."

Miss Emy's shoulders fell a little, but she straightened them up again. "Animals are real, not a wispy ghost spirit," Miss Emy said.

Paul put the peanut butter in the trap. "My friend's got a couple of snakes. He'll feed the rat to it."

"What kind of friend has snakes?" Miss Emy asked, shivering all over.

"A friend with snakes," Paul said. He laughed. "He's a man I work with over at the plant, and he just likes snakes, I guess. They're not poisonous. They're constrictors, a different kind of snakes, not from around here."

"Fine, just catch the rats," she said.

As they grew, the girls began sleeping in their own bedroom, and drifted away from their mother. Miss Emy knew they stayed up all night reading, telling stories, and making web catchers. For the most part, the nightmares lessened and faded. She melted into the whole bed and across the body of her husband freely for the first time since their children had been born.

They developed like that for years in the city. The girls played instruments and sports. School buses snapped them up in the morning and spit them out that afternoon. The neighbors' houses lined up around theirs. The children rode their bicycles in an abandoned lot at the corner of the block. In the other direction, they walked to the church on Sunday mornings with heels ticking on the sidewalks.

Miss Emy had always been resourceful enough to sew her own clothes and curtains. In Granville, she ordered good fabric from catalogues, and it was often not what she expected or was too expensive. She used the skeins of cotton and wool dyed in pokeberry stain by Paul's sister, Cora. She crocheted in reds and purples from the pokeberry mixtures that were never the same coloring, depending on how much vinegar Cora had used to make the dye baths and how long she'd soaked the fabrics. In Nashville, Miss Emy started a little business that thrived. Paul bought a newer sewing machine from Sears and Roebuck. She couldn't pump the pedal fast enough, sewing summer dresses for the children from church, and she taught quite a few of her friends there how to sew, too. Miss Emy used smocking to make images of balloons, animals, letters, initials, or whatever the mothers wanted. Even Mrs. Clark commissioned new drapes for her windows. All the fabric stores offered up a rainbow of colors and hundreds of patterns. And, thanks to Jackie Kennedy, the designs for women were fashionably straight and plain. Luckily, Miss Emy fit the fashion. She was skinny and promoted the A-line.

It was the first time Miss Emy felt good about her body's thin frame. "You don't seem to belong to those children," the church secretary said when she ordered a christening gown. "I mean, they're adorable, earthy girls. I just couldn't believe you were their mother at first." Twiggy didn't make the scene for almost six more years, but eventually, Miss Emy would be complimented, "You look just like Twiggy to me." Miss Emy didn't feel resentment for her lack of curves for the first time. While the girls were natural hills, she was the long lines of plains.

She went less and less to Granville as the years passed, but managed to return for the holidays, at least the big ones. The girls went every summer for five years. She couldn't apply her resistance to Zona and Hoot's religion to the girls' view of them. Miss Emy continued to encourage education to counterbalance superstition, believing books had the answers without condemning their grandparents. But during junior high, it was roller-skating that distracted them away from Nowheresville.

The girls ate sour candy and roller-skated constantly with a spinning record or 8-track blaring in their house if the rink wasn't open. On the weekends, the wooden table with their names carved into it awaited. It was two blocks away so they skated there or biked in the case of rain. And they wanted their clothes skimpier. Miss Emy taught them how to sew their own halter and tube tops. They couldn't master the pants, which had to be cut low on the hips and tight. Paul didn't like it at all. He said she needed to pay more attention to them, but Miss Emy assured him that she wasn't intimidated after seeing their crowd at the dinky roller-skating rink tables. They were kids having their own good time.

Truthfully, it was partially an excuse. Miss Emy wanted to keep the change from Nowheresville in her life spinning round and round, and Paul had already hinted that they might consider moving back to Granville because the racial tension in Nashville was escalating. The freedom rides had started and headed into Alabama, getting stopped in Gadsden. The lunch counter sit-ins ramped up the momentum, and Miss Emy experienced first-hand what it looks like when the National Guard enters to "keep the peace."

In the '60s in Nashville, there wasn't an interstate exit at Charlotte Pike or 46th Avenue. When he drove the family from Granville, Paul exited close to the Tennessee State University campus, where the racial tensions in Nashville reached the height of action. The students were ready to fight for racial freedom. They were ready to move forward. Paul's car passed alongside the TSU campus, where the students prepared for a protest, lining up to organize. Miss Emy ducked down in the seat, saying, "What if they hate me because I'm so white?"

Paul was as dark as a Cherokee, and no one bothered him. He argued that she should "sit up and act right." The traffic slowed while students ran across the street, laughing, joking, some singing with their arms linked together. Someone threw a small rock at the window after noticing Miss Emy peek through the window to watch everything. She raised her frightened eyes again and caught the attention of more people. A few students banged against the window glass. They shouted close to the window, "We're the same as you! We deserve the same freedoms!" Miss Emy slid onto the floorboards. "Daddy," both of the girls called uncertainly and hugged each other in the backseat.

Paul gave a stern look out the window, beeped his horn in a little rhythm and smiled. He waved. After a few rounds, the students began to clap along with his rhythm and move to the side so that he could continue to pass. Miss Emy sat up in her seat, she clapped, and she smiled. Everything shifted. That moment changed her life, and Miss Emy always said, "It's your attitude that will change things. Don't have fear on your heart. Have unity in your heart."

Miss Emy marched down Jefferson Street. She didn't shy away, no, Miss Emy put her little white self in the middle of it all. She was determined not to leave the city. Paul worried about the effects on the children. He worried about escalating violence in the schools. He worried about his little girls, no matter how he felt inside. And after President Kennedy was shot, Miss Emy began to worry alongside him. She fretted daily about what would happen to the country if people were continually denied their freedoms.

The troubles with Carolyn were an easy excuse for them to leave. They were having problems from her before going to Granville for Christmas vacation and her 13th birthday. Melinda wore flower patches on her pants and wrote poetry about stars and flowers. Miss Emy knew that the social atmosphere would eventually catch up to her intellectual ways. In the meantime, Carolyn took more liberties by sneaking out the window of her room. Although Miss Emy suspected the activity was more frequent, she caught her two different times missing in the morning. What shocked Miss Emy is that Carolyn fell back on the old sleepwalking and nightmares excuse. Miss Emy believed her the first time because she was good at trembling with a dazed stare as if she had been in a far-off spirit land. That's the trash she told Miss Emy, too. After the second time, Miss Emy knew it was really a boy and decided their family needed the seclusion of a long Christmas break on the farm. Paul had vacation time. And besides, it had been a whole year since Miss Emy had gone back to Nowheresville, the longest time she'd ever stayed away.

The night before they left, Miss Emy had the only dream she could really remember in her life. She prided herself on getting a good night's sleep and not being a big dreamer. In the dream, Miss Emy was walking fast through the woods in the dark. It was like she was running from somebody, but she didn't know who. It was hard for her to remember the little things from the dream, but she finally reached the edge of this lake or big pond. All these women sat around it with their feet dangling in the water. They paddled their feet, and little bubbles formed and floated out into the center of the lake. When Miss Emy got closer, she noticed that kittens were in those bubbles. They were all orange, and some had stripes. The women asked her if she wanted to paddle. Miss Emy told them she would wait until it was brighter outside. As she walked around the edge of the water, she watched the red and blue birds playing in the trees. Before she got all the way around, she woke up. In the dream, she kept thinking *why are the birds out at night* and *I have to make it all the way around.* Miss Emy never liked dreams and this one bugged her all day, especially since they were leaving for Granville.

When they arrived at the farm, Hoot stood in front of the big woodstove in the kitchen, warming his skinny hands. His hair had turned all silver finally. He helped the girls with the rest of their things while Miss Emy found Zona in the bedroom, spreading a sheet over the bed. There wasn't a strand of white in her hair. It was wound neatly into a circled braid. Her body didn't even look that much older and she was sixty. Miss Emy put her suitcases in the corner and wanted to crawl into that bed already. The drive made her feel dazed and she stood at the foot of the bed staring out the window beside it. Miss Emy heard herself explaining that she was tired and she began telling Zona about the dream. Her body swayed and she felt Zona's hand on the small of her back. Then, another pressed gently into her stomach.

"It'll be just a second, honey," Zona said from beside her and guided Miss Emy out of the way. "I'll have it ready for you. You can stay right here."

Miss Emy noticed Zona's silver ring on the pinkie finger that was on her stomach when she scooted Miss Emy to the side. It seemed plain and Miss Emy wondered why Zona had worn it all these years.

"Sure is nice to see you," Zona said and moved around the bed. "There's some food waiting by the stove if you want it. You might find it before the others get to it first."

Miss Emy thanked her and walked away.

"It's always better when you eat with your feet propped up," Zona said as Miss Emy moved through the doorway.

"I'll try that," Miss Emy said. At least Zona was wittier in old age even if Miss Emy didn't see the years any more than a few wrinkles around the corners of her eyes. In the brighter days that passed, Miss Emy noticed the shiny spool of gray threaded into her braid.

****

They returned to Nashville after uneventful holidays. Miss Emy didn't get the intention of Zona's advice for two months. And then, it rang in her ears when the doctor said, "Looks like you have a little one on the way. That's the good news anyway." He shuffled through the papers in her chart and all Miss Emy could do was look at the traffic out the window. The trees of the park stood gray and naked along the street.

"And the bad news?" she asked.

"Because of your small size, your cervix is too thin," he said. "That means bed rest. Do you have someone who can take care of you?"

"But my size wasn't a problem before. I've always been the same size."

"Age has caught up to you," he said. "How old were you when you had your other children?"

"Eighteen and twenty," she said. "What do you mean by bed rest?"

"You are thirty-two now. That makes a difference with your small size," he said and stopped to blow his nose. "You may only get out of bed for bathing and going to the restroom. If you walk too much, you could induce labor."

"How much is too much?"

"That's what I'm telling you," he said. "Anything more than the restroom could be too much. I'm recommending that you eat more and remain in a reclining state as much as possible. Is there someone who can care for you?"

"I'll work it out," Miss Emy said.

"You'll be able to put your feet up?" he asked and that's when she recalled Zona's witty remark. He fanned the chart with his thumb. "And eat more?" He kept staring at her.

Miss Emy nodded, but she was uncertain about what to do.

She was scared of hurting herself, of losing the baby, of being pregnant all over again. Paul bit the corner of his lip to hide the smile when she talked to him that evening. The girls said that they would take care of her, but school was more important to Miss Emy. They didn't know how to care for someone, and the sly grin on Carolyn's face revealed that she would surely take advantage of the orders for Miss Emy's bed rest.

Paul confirmed what had been ripening in her mind. "You could go back to the farm until after the baby's born. Mama would help you. Or Dad if you can't settle on the thought of Mama caring for you."

Miss Emy never made a decision so quickly and clearly. She was more stunned over her own feelings than the pregnancy itself. She was going back to Nowheresville with the girls, but they weren't happy about it. Paul would be alone during the week again; at least, he was never one to complain about changes. Maybe he worked too much to worry. In two weeks' time from seeing the doctor in Nashville, Miss Emy was back in Granville with two hateful, tear-streaked girls.

"I didn't have any other choice," she said to them. "You have to go to school and I didn't want to burden you with caring for me all the time."

"And where's Dad in all this?" Carolyn asked. "He gets to do what he wants and stay at home. And if we have to go to school anyway and you don't want to burden us, then why can't we stay with Dad?" Even though Granville had grown a little, the girls didn't have the same activities to occupy their time. For Carolyn, sneaking out of the house wasn't as much fun when she lived miles away from anyone except Hoot and Zona.

"Your father works!" Miss Emy shouted. "Like he wants to work all of the time. And he drives back here on the weekends to work more. For what?" she asked. They rolled their eyes at her. "I'm not staying here by myself. And yes, I need your help sometimes. Your Ma Zona can't do everything."

"After the way you've always treated her, I don't know why she takes care of you anyway," Melinda said. "What have you ever done for her?"

"If she has a problem with me, she can ask that question herself." Miss Emy stared hard at them. That's when they heard Zona moving in the kitchen and knew she was listening. The clock did show dinnertime. They didn't talk any more than they used to, but Zona spent most of the days with Miss Emy and made all her meals.

Living there again didn't solve all of their problems. At first, Miss Emy was okay with her decision, made the best of it when faced with the girls or when Paul visited weekends. But while spring grew hot and thick outside her window, Miss Emy swelled with loneliness. Paul forwarded all her magazines and Hoot moved the television into her bedroom, but nothing soothed her agitation. It wasn't fun the first two times, but Miss Emy never had a pregnancy so uncomfortable.

When the girls tried to make up for their differences, they lit Miss Emy's fuse instead. They came into the room all proud and serious.

"We're sorry," Carolyn said. "We've made you a present and want to do something fun and nice for you."

Melinda said, "Maybe it will cheer you up," and, "Just be open-minded."

Carolyn placed a candle on the table and instructed Miss Emy to move to one side of the bed. Carolyn unfolded a piece of thin, pokeberry-dyed cloth with tiny flowers and tigers stitched around the edges.

"That's pretty," Miss Emy said.

"Ma Zona made it and gave it to me," Melinda said. "Both of us made these." She removed a stack of large cards and handed the cloth to Miss Emy. The glittery cards spread in a rainbow across the bed. Then, Miss Emy saw the black bird, but it was a red bird this time, carrying a black fish whose glittery scales flaked into the folds of the cover.

"Why do you have these?" she asked and pushed the cards away, remembering Jane's son.

"Mom, I told you to be open-minded!" Melinda shouted.

"You need to be minding your own business, making something useful, doing something constructive. Not this superstitious nonsense. Enough is enough." Miss Emy ripped one of the cards.

"They're based on stars and planets, not superstitions," Carolyn said, grabbing the other cards quickly. After that, they moved all their things up to Hoot and Zona's house. Miss Emy was incensed, but felt powerless to stop them. She listened to Hoot's advice and believed him when he told her that her girls would be back, just give them some time.

And then, there was Hazel. She sure didn't help when she visited from Detroit. They wrote letters back and forth through the years. Miss Emy saw her once for New Year's Day after they moved, but Miss Emy was convinced that her surprise stay during the pregnancy was an opportunity to gloat. Luke owned some rental properties in Detroit. She had finally gone to college and worked as a nurse in a big, regional hospital. Hazel's pictures spread across Miss Emy's legs on the bed and revealed them laughing with all the bigwigs in town.

"And, I introduced Luke to one of the builders. His daughter was one of my patients, and I helped take care of her through an operation," Hazel said and pointed to a picture that was sliding off Miss Emy's leg. Wearing a suit and hard hat, Luke stood in front of a building surrounded by bulldozers with two other smiling men in suits and hard hats. "Luke got to be involved with all these city planners," she said. "He was the supervising electrician for a new building project."

"Hazel, can you move these pictures?" Miss Emy said, picking up the one before it fell. "I feel like I can't move. You've got me all blocked in here."

"I can tell you only have a couple months to go," she said scooping up the pictures. She took the one from Miss Emy's hand. "You sure are testy," she said. She sized up her friend's swollen stomach. "I guess I would be, too. Of course, I can't say I know how you feel. You're lucky to have children." Hazel stacked the pictures, her face turning red, as if she could cry. "I'm just trying to entertain you a little with something different."

Miss Emy asked for a picture of her and Luke to put on the dresser mirror. That made Hazel happy. When she left that afternoon, Miss Emy asked Zona to take it down and put it in the album. She didn't write Hazel for a long time after that. She didn't know what to say and tried to avoid thinking about her. Miss Emy's jealous emotions germinated and she struggled with anger in silence.

Wearing slouchy clothes was dreary. It was too hot to sit outside. The bed was formed to her body and the view had grown old. Her thoughts were hot underneath the surface. Irritation bubbled all over her skin some days. She hated the drive in to the tiny hospital in town to see the doctor for her weekly exam. Luckily, the town had grown and needed two new doctors, and one of them became her obstetrician after she moved. Hoot insisted upon carrying her to the truck and placing her onto the seat, then pushing her in a wheelchair down the hospital corridors. Zona and the girls had brushed her hair and pinned it with flowers through the whole pregnancy, soothing her in the beginning. But in the late pregnancy, all the touching caused her to cringe inside—the doctor, Hoot, Zona, her children, even her husband when he visited. Miss Emy didn't want anyone near her body, much less someone touching her, even in the slightest way. She snapped at Zona, who immediately sent Hoot as her replacement. He and Miss Emy had an understanding to ignore one another unless he was delivering something. Then, they stuck with the pleasantries of *please, thank you,* and *you're welcome.* By the night that her contractions surprised Miss Emy, she had already resolved to deliver the baby by herself or be carried off to the hospital.

Because the moon was in Pisces, Hoot had fried fish for dinner. The smell stuck to everything and made Miss Emy nauseated. She couldn't eat it and told him to just let her sleep. It was completely dark when the contractions finally got the better of her tossing in bed. The frog croaks and cricket chirps covered up her grunts as she struggled to prop a pillow behind her back and sit up a little so she could catch her breath. She didn't even hear Zona in the house. Miss Emy saw Zona's silver-ringed hand holding the base of the oil lamp that she set on the table. When Zona turned the dial, Miss Emy could see the sweat soaking through her thin pants and t-shirt. Zona moved the fan into the window, and the warm air pulled through Miss Emy's sticky hair. The draft smelled like fish and mint.

"First thing we got to do, honey, is wash your hair," Zona said. "There's a bath ready for you. It's warm but you soak in that until you have to add the cool water."

The scent of the mint became stronger in the bathroom. Three little red candles were lit on the back of the toilet. Green leaves and flowers floated on top of the bath, glinting in the fragments of light from the candle. Hanging from the faucet, a bundle of sliced plants, bark, and sticks dangled and dipped into the water. The pain Miss Emy felt was as tight as the string around those plants, and she couldn't consider allowing someone to place her in a truck so that she could ride into that tiny, dingy hospital. Her contractions flared and flickered with the candles. After she managed to undress, her muscles throbbed from the lack of activity over the past months. Her reflection in the mirror faltered. She blew those three candles out, closed the door, and sank into the water. The darkness wrapped her up and blanketed her fears. She held onto sharp aches in the steam of that motionless room. She wanted to intensify her pain and suffocate in it. When she dunked her head under, Zona opened the door. She turned on the cool water, poured something from a bottle into her hand, and pushed her fingers into Miss Emy's hair.

"I don't understand you people," Miss Emy said. Zona's nails scratched over her scalp.

"We're all born from the same mother," Zona said and whirled the foam up into a point.

"Well, don't make that music at me like you did during the first two deliveries."

"Fine, but it makes the body release the baby easier. That's my belief."

Miss Emy's pain suddenly swelled inside and she held onto her abdomen. She moaned.

"When you let go, the musical instruments carry you through the pain. The fingers and hands playing those instruments are coaxing life forward, telling your body to use the rhythm, telling the baby to hear us celebrate her life."

The cool water curled around Miss Emy's toes and climbed up her legs. When it began to hug Miss Emy's hips and stomach, Zona turned off the faucet.

"I understand that your family wants to welcome the baby, but we all have our ways. I want to listen to the room, to myself, to hear the birth for what it is, and it could be quiet sometimes," Miss Emy said.

"Not to worry," Zona said, scratching Miss Emy's scalp again. "Now, wash that out, child." Zona turned away from Miss Emy and said, "I must light these candles and move them into the room. I changed the bed for you."

Miss Emy looked at her closely, like she was a different person. Certainly, she wasn't the same Zona that Miss Emy had known all these years.

After Miss Emy made it back to bed, everything happened faster than she could remember. Zona checked Miss Emy's progress swiftly and broke her waters with a small hook on her fingertip. When the sun came up that August morning, Miss Emy made her eyes follow the cardinals and blue jays outside the window while her mouth screamed and cried and apologized. She puffed forth heavy, hot, salty breaths while the sweat washed over her scalp. She cried in little whispered pleading melodies during some contractions. She knitted her toes and fingers and rubbed her feet back and forth. Her body opened up for a third time to life, forcing her baby out into the world. By lunchtime, Miss Emy held a squalling child. Zona wiped Miss Emy's hair back with a wet rag. Miss Emy's body was numb but she was alert for the first time. The fan in the window spun the sunlight around in chopped up circles.

"Miss Emy, you sure did surprise me with your strength, especially to be such a little woman," Zona said. "Hoot and the girls are waiting for me to call them to come down here." Then, she looked at the baby and said, "You were a stubborn pain, and I hope you don't cause too much trouble with your life. But I don't know...." She patted Miss Emy's shoulder. "Paul should be on his way from Nashville by now."

"You've got older sisters," Miss Emy said to the baby, who would not stop crying. She bounced and cuddled but it didn't matter. "Don't you want to meet them?"

Zona left the room to call up to the other house. The baby went quiet when Miss Emy wiped its face with the washcloth Zona had left on her head.

"They must be on their way," Zona said, returning to the room. "The girls are planning to move back in and help out with their little brother."

"How do you know all of these things, Zona?" Miss Emy asked. "I don't understand."

Zona flared out a sheet, let it billow and drop over Miss Emy's legs.

"How did you know I'd have the baby last night?" Miss Emy asked. The baby squirmed. Zona took the washcloth and dipped it in a bowl of water beside the bed. "I'm not due for another month, at least," Miss Emy said. Zona gave the washcloth to Miss Emy.

"I remember the little things," Zona said. A draft snapped the door shut, and they heard Hoot and the girls walking from the kitchen. They smelled Hoot's cigar. Miss Emy and Zona grinned at each other while listening to the girls place last bets on whether it was a girl or boy. As soon as they opened the door, he started squalling again.

CHAPTER 2

ASSIGNMENT TWO

After I got Miss Emy's story about becoming a mother, I turned it in for the class. I wrote more than I had ever written in my life for that assignment. I tried to get down every detail. I didn't want to miss a thing since our professor emphasized the need for details that will connect into greater meaning as the story progresses. By that time, we all knew that we'd be sticking to this way of digging into our family's place in the world, and some psychology as well. During some of the classes, we listened to our peers read from self-involved drafts about their dating dramas or crazy relatives instead of understanding where the story of their lives was actually happening. I wanted my family's story to be enjoyable, or else I'd cringe thinking that my classmates were bored by what I'd written.

For the next assignment, our English professor said, "Now that you've collected a story about your family's time and place and, hopefully, development, let's keep going with this as a class. For the next assignment, go find someone and ask about your family's economics. What products, companies, or trades are connected to your family? You may have discovered something about this in the first assignment, but let's focus on specifics for this writing assignment. Based on what I've learned from all of you in your in-class free-writes, everyone in this class has access to family members who have agreed to interviews for these assignments." During class, she didn't say much more as far as instructions or lectures; instead she asked us to read from our work. Then, our classmates would give feedback about how to make our stories better and what parts were unclear or confusing. After that, the professor would make suggestions on how we could satisfy our "readers", and by that, she meant our classmates. I didn't realize that I was becoming a writer in the process.

Some memories are a quick fire flash—deliberate. They go straight for the moments when you aren't expecting anything—during sleep, the middle of a book, zoned out during a test, parked at a red light waiting and staring at other drivers, or listening to music—almost anything can trigger the sudden flash of a memory when it wants to be let loose. I learned that these are the best moments to write down on paper. They come in quickly and create a flare, on the page, too. If I didn't write it down, sometimes I couldn't ever remember it in the same way. One of my memories that flared up during the course of the class involved fire—real flames.

There I was, in the salon after class, wondering what I would write about for the next assignment, reclined and staring at a large, blown-up photograph stuck to the ceiling of a sunrise between mountain peaks, when the memory overtook me. My hairstylist pinned pictures and posters with motivational aspirations to the ceiling above the sinks, since the customers have their heads back while she scrubs, massages, and conditions. This mountain sunrise scene dared, "Don't let life pass you by! Dream for adventure!" The hairstylist twisted my hair and wrapped it in a towel. I was trying to hide my tears, but she noticed. "Am I pulling your hair too much?" she asked.

"It's okay," I said. "I just remembered something that I haven't thought about in twenty years...since it happened. Crazy when some memory like that comes back all of a sudden, for no reason, and then, you think about all the stuff that's happened in your life since that time." I sighed, thinking of how much wonder I have about the tragedies and remedies. I didn't have many memories of my Dad that didn't involve heroin, rehabs, the drama of women, junkies, and drug dealers, and his living on the street as I got older. Those memories go so quickly, as if buzzing with honey, loaded with the heaviness of dying clover ruffles in the heat of summer, and they sting like a hornet. I suddenly remembered when my Dad set fire to honey whiskey on peaches. Mine were sprinkled with cinnamon, and the flame went up around the peaches in a wild flicker, blue and orange, the yellow peach shriveling soft, glowing, and my Dad's breath pushing a wave of smoke after the flame was extinguished. He added a spoonful of whipped cream I helped to fluff up with the handheld mixer.

I felt that instant of joy in my past, and the memory caused me to cry with anger. I couldn't face the family economics given by my Dad for this assignment, not just yet, even if I was getting closer. I went backward first, where it felt entertaining to be in someone else's memories and old timey drama.

****

I learned that my great-granddaddy, Hoot, was a writer, but he didn't share his writings with others. He kept journals and daily remarks about his family and thoughts about business and progress, even spirituality and moonshine recipes, but they were private. Each of my aunts and my Daddy, my grandma Miss Emy, and Aunt Cora, have confirmed that Hoot wrote in his journals every day. Some people even say he kept peoples' secrets in the notebooks, just in case he needed some blackmail material on them; though I've never met anyone who confessed that Hoot blackmailed people. Most everything my family told about Hoot was gossip and speculation.

His more public talent was moonshining and he knew the creeks and hollows, the coil and flow, that sweet mixture and sting better than anyone...and, I'll prove it to you in a revelation before long, but we can't get ahead of the story. Hoot would want to have his talk, and his surviving papers from the journals will have to suffice.

They all have talents, but those journals could reveal the truth about Zona and so many tales that need to be known. She's my great-grandma, Hoot's wife, the town midwife, who was supposedly the daughter of a ruffian rambler and mixed race Native American farm girl, mother to Cora and many other children, including my paternal grandpa, Paul. She delivered my Dad in the family farmhouse, on land that dates back to a federal land grant given to my great-great-great-great grandfather for time spent fighting in the Revolutionary War. As the only son born to Colonel Ballard and Nenny, Hoot ended up keeping the land and farming it, and moonshining to make cash money, while his sister, Rose, married a lawyer and moved into town. He didn't write often about her. Great Aunt Cora gave me a few of the papers she found in an old Bible that belonged to her father, Hoot. I went to visit my Great Aunt Cora regularly once she had her knees replaced and moved in with my aunt, Melinda.

Hoot Ballard's Writings, 1919-1927

On the first page I opened, Hoot was saying that the ripe summer was the best time to sell whiskey: *The blanketed summertime wrapped around people, stifling them so they needed a nip to kick back and take their clothes off without worrying so much, jump in the cool creek in a wet shirt, strip off a sticky day and skinny dip in cold water. Find the mossiest, coolest stone to rest your tired limbs from the summer work. The bees busied and frenzied, and getting heavy, the honey ready to lay right in that mixture of shine and pleasure the tongue.*

"I know my herbs better than any other shiner," Hoot prided himself further down the page. *"Maybe the herbalist in me is the strongest one. Zona says it's so—that my tinctures and soaking mixtures ease the labor pains and help the women to breathe between spasms. I planted the medicine wheel with Zona, the way our mothers taught us, each with her own method, and we combined the two, as we have learned to do since we met."*

I was in awe of their connection. Before the papers, I didn't understand their relationship. To so many relatives, Zona was domineering and Hoot was gently, albeit persistently, completing work that didn't seem like work. Something about him was comical in the descriptions from my aunts, but I lost that impression when I received the journal pages from Cora and understood her impressions of her father. Hoot was a complicated man—master moonshiner, herbalist, child to a couple of rough mystics.

The Ballard land was from the land grant, and it's the site of pastures as well as a meteorite impact crater. So something mysterious has existed on the farm since prehistoric times. The rippling valleys from that ancient impact allowed Hoot to have ample cool, running creeks and streams deep in the valleys for making moonshine, along with high fields for cattle and planting crops like tobacco, corn, potatoes, and sugar cane. He and Zona had plenty of sons to tend and manage it all.

Driving back into that land, winding through the roads, I chase after their shadows, the previous lives of my ancestors—their secrets and dreams. Twisting through, into the limestone-banked woodlands, it's like some doorway opens up to only those who know it, a caney fork in the land and you've got to choose the right direction, back into this other world, where you can learn about the spirits and the ways of the shadows—the ways of earth magic. The road jumps up and up, climbing out of and plunging back inside the hills; the grapevine drips down from the tree canopy, and you can't see the floor of the forests from the top of the ridgeline. The hills ripple into sharp points along every horizon. The river is slow and steady and easy in these hills, but deep. It goes down into pure coldness, even when you leave it, pushing into the next little valley, threaded and sewed and pulled together, and you feel that coldness rise up from the shadows, circle into the car suddenly through the ninety-degree heat, through the hundred-percent humidity on the top of green fields. You know some spirit carried the chill up there to you, so you follow the cold currents of the spirits back to where you belong.

And, I chose to go in search for those stories found in the forests and fields where my family roamed, chose to chase that cold history every chance I got. I knew secrets existed, and the lost journals held parts of them. Aunt Cora was another part, but I felt the missing pieces, the mysteries that they weren't communicating and that I would never find even as my heart longed for them with each beat and my head perched itself to scour for clues in dreams and desires, in books and library archives. I asked

Aunt Cora why she gave me the papers she found in Hoot's Bible. I questioned her about why only a few pages were folded and placed in a Bible, and what could have happened to the notebooks, the leather-bound journals, and the little pads of paper that my relatives say he had accumulated over the years and locked in a bureau in his bedroom. I'm suspicious that Aunt Cora had the journals at one time, even if she doesn't want to admit it now. The papers look like they came from at least two different journals.

1924

When I was eighteen, I married a poor, but strong Indian girl, Arizona, the one called Zona. We have many sons and farming comes naturally to Zona, as does midwifery. Fortune has shined on us with fertile generosity.

The next set of pages didn't have a date and a few of the words were faded and creased so badly, I had to guess. This is what I think it said, based on what I could read:

"And in respect, we are fair in service to others. My reputation is one of honest judgment and a fair price. I won't allow my boys to take extra pay, and I check up on them enough to know that they never take more than the selling price, even when the purchasers insist.

I have three stills back in my hills. I don't understand the judgment against it. If you want to abstain from drinking it, do as you like, but to insist that other men follow your way is not the Providence of this Country. I am not a mean man, and I have heard that some men can become the devil's accomplice under the sting of the shine, but I think those men have meanness in themselves already."

The next paper was torn in a few places, but the words were remarkably legible, as was the date.

April 26, 1924

The pokeberry bush makes a smart mess of greens, and we are covered in it here on the Ridge. The proliferation of it on our property makes me proud. The depth and fertility of the forest and pastures draw me in, and I am in wonder of the way all the plants benefit one another. Growing is my way of life.

I especially like the history of the land and our farm. A modest home, but it is the stories within it that make the deal. Great-grandfather fought in the Revolutionary War and entered Tennessee from Virginia. He married an Indian, and I guess you could say that I did, too. Zona says that one of her grandmothers had white hair and eyes blue as forget-me-nots. Zona did not inherit her grandmother's appearance, but she did retain a few powder horns, arrowheads, spear tips, blankets, and hides. This place is our family's legacy. These hollows are dug into the earth, and it is not an easy place to breach, so we have been left alone, left to trade and conduct commerce in our own quiet way. It has not always been easy, but there is a way of being that allows you in, and for knowing that the others have secrets in them, too. Look them right in the eye, because you know it is a truth. It is also a blessing to have so many sons, for the might of us and for cultivating the land.

I found a small set of pages folded inside the larger journal pages, and they were torn in a few places, but contained a dialogue that he copied down about one of his main business customers in bootlegging:

...and making whiskey. I sell shine, but the whiskey I make for myself reminds me of why I am in this business. I will not allow just anybody to drink my best sipping whiskey. No, only if a man comes out here to visit me on my farm, to sit at my table, in my office, do I permit him to have a drink of my drink, and then he can get his fill. If he is a buying man of his word. My sons and my son-in-law, three of them, drive shine up to Chicago and then, make fast to Detroit. It took me just one visit from one man to close the deal, and after he sat at my table and drank until the hills gleamed with their green twinkling with fireflies, winking and winning him over, and that one field of wheat swayed in golden folds, he said, "I like you, Hoot Ballard. I definitely do. Let your boys ride."

The pokeberry bush, fortuitous plant, served as a point of intrigue for my esteemed guest.

"What are these letters here?" he pointed and tapped on the glass to the cabinet. "Are these some secret Indian code or something? Why are they that color?"

"These are from the Civil War," I told him. He is a Yankee, a boss, so I had to explain. I said, "When my great uncles were out fighting, they wrote letters back home using pokeberries and a turkey feather as a pen."

The man laughed. "What's a pokeberry?"

"It's a small purple berry that grows on a pokeberry bush."

"What do they taste like?"

"No one eats the berries. We cook the leaves and fry up the shoots. They're tender and not quite as bitter as those from turnips."

He was quite impressed by our resourcefulness and good taste, especially after dinner. He is a gentleman.

CHAPTER 3

ASSIGNMENT THREE

For the third assignment, the professor said, "Find out something juicy. Romance. Betrayal. Both. Ask one of your relatives about their first love. Romance is a hot topic with everyone. We all need love, or at least lust, in our lives." She laughed. "You might be surprised by what you find out." I could visit other relatives, but I wanted to know more about the old time history of my immediate family. I went back to my Great Aunt Cora, and the professor was right, romance is a hot topic.

Great Aunt Cora, 1920

It wasn't a perfect summer everywhere, but it *was* on the Ballard farm, according to Cora. That spring the house arrived on the train, straight from Sears and Roebuck, and Cora's whole family—brothers, cousins, friends, even some distant relatives—and their neighbors helped with the assembly on top of the cellar and foundation that Hoot and his oldest sons had already made. The community's participation lasted all of two days, but the building of the Ballard home continued with piping, wiring, ventilating, fixing, adorning, and decorating for months, and truly, lifetimes.

Cora didn't ever leave except twice a year for the two biggest events in town, and now with a kitchen as an actual room in the house—a room that she heated to life and into which she brought all of the bounty from the garden and field and river—she wasn't as focused on the expectations of those two events that summer. She went to the fair for one day on the other side of the county. It like to wore her out riding that far, even though she was so excited when they left that morning. The second event was the Poke Sallet Festival, and Granville celebrated the plant every year in town. Maybe it went back to the Shawnee and the Cherokee, tribes who lived in the area before the settlers, maybe it was about survival of both cultures in some way, or maybe it just stuck and flourished as weeds do, in spite of what people wanted, and they made the most out of it—to eat and to celebrate. They planted roses, hydrangeas, apple trees, wisteria, lilies, snowball bushes, and every manner of ruffle and frill around their houses, and tobacco, corn, sugar cane, and later, soybeans, in the fields, with their own messes of turnips, potatoes, beets, melons, beans, squash, zucchini, eggplant, and everything that grows standard for a household with a dozen family members and overflowing.

That spring at the Poke Sallet Festival, Cora noticed Harold Flynn at first sight and couldn't seem to take her eyes off of him, and he nearly fell over while staring at her before the cake walk. He bumped into her and said, "Dance with me, Cora?" She blushed and put her hand in his. He was tan and shorter than her brothers, but his square legs seemed to anchor onto the floor and moved her gracefully in dance at the same time. She could look straight into his eyes when he pulled her close to his body, and she felt matched to him. His hair was almost white from being outdoors, and the sun had taken his eyebrows and left a blonde blaze in their place across his brow that made his green eyes light up as bold as spring. His eyes were joyous, Cora thought. They danced together and giggled, but didn't dare say a word to one another for fear of saying the wrong thing. Cora thought that if he brushed close to her again, she would need someone to bring her a chair before her knees gave out altogether. He finally spoke and said that he had been in Kentucky for a while, apprenticing as a farrier, but he had plans to come back to Granville and work with the walking horses at Gentry's Stables.

Cora said, "I thought you were going to college."

And he said, "Miss Cora, don't you listen to any gossip around town with your friends?"

"All I got is a bunch of brothers," Cora said. "Except for Jane, and she's too busy flying all over the place to listen."

When he laughed, he smirked at the end, looked at Cora out of the corner of his eye, as if he could see every room of her innocence, and how much more advanced Jane was even though she was the younger sister. Jane just understood boys better than Cora did. She understood people and knew how to manipulate and woo them. Their Mama, Zona, said, "Jane can read people like a book. That's something you don't know how to do, Cora. Your sister could teach you a few things if you had a mind to listen."

Cora liked to listen to jokes or to watch people act silly. She noticed exactly how to make a pie or to cook the best greens just after seeing someone do it one time. She knew just how much to put in the pastry to make a sturdy, flaky side pie, and she could adapt depending on the grind of flour and the coarseness of the sugar, the thickness of honey or molasses. That's what she knew, and even if Zona ate all of Cora's food and smacked her lips, Zona didn't think there was nothing to her skill. In Zona's mind, Cora didn't know anything if she couldn't work in the field, deliver babies, or read peoples' motives.

"Only thing you're good at is shoving food in folks' mouths to make them shut up," Zona said at the kitchen table one evening.

Hoot said, "And they love it, Cora. That's something." He winked at his daughter.

Zona couldn't resist bringing up Hoot's moonshine-making as a similarity to Cora's cooking, "You just see it that way 'cause that's what you do, too, in a manner of speaking."

"Only my product does make some men blather on and on after they've filled their mouths to the rim." He slapped his knee and chuckled. "You ever pondered that?" he asked Zona. "I suppose you have, since pondering is what you do best."

She smirked and took a pronounced gaze around the table at all of the boys and their sturdy shoulders. She took responsibility for those boys, who would be men, and she never let Hoot forget where his work force originated. Brothers. All of those brown eyes, brown heads, those eyelids closing fast in the evenings after an initial gallop and run, a wrestling ring in the dust, brushing the horses, walking to the pond to bathe, someone going in the other direction to the hot spring, sitting on the porch, plucking strings, plucking feathers, setting up the pans for the morning, rolling out the dough, smoking and finding a quilt, lighting the lamp, reading and being reminded to snuff it out or someone would eventually come along and blow your light out just because he felt like it.

At the Poke Sallet Festival, Harold said, nervously, "I've almost finished my apprenticeship." He smiled confidently, the dimple in his chin showed itself. He didn't seem like the thin boys Cora knew. Even if they were long-legged, they still didn't look strong like he did. She looked him over in those moments of dancing and absorbed the details—the mole beside his ear, the way his ear lobes were attached to the skin of his neck, the scars on his forearms, the calluses on his fingers and thumbs, the boyish flinch and grin when her thigh brushed against his during their dance.

"You still living out on your parents' place, aren't you? Everybody's talking about the new house, and I'm sorry I couldn't be there to help with construction," he said.

She nodded, trying to catch her breath after the fast song the band was playing.

"I was around there yesterday and didn't see you at all," he said. "Beautiful gabling around the porch, and the craftsmanship of the wood on the front door and in the kitchen surprised me."

"I was staying with my cousins in town last night—on account of the festival today," she said, glancing around so she could introduce Harold to Elizabeth, her older cousin who was about his age; but right about that time, Cora had a realization—one of the rare times when she did a good job of reading someone without their saying anything—she felt his eyes staring at her lips. He licked his own lips and smiled. Cora blushed and moved uncomfortably, and she decided that she wasn't going to introduce him to her cousin. She pulled at the bow tied on the side of her dress. She looked down at her breasts, wishing they were like Jane's and feeling self-conscious by her small size all of a sudden. She thought they'd grow when she turned fourteen, but they were still small when she was sixteen. Jane's were giant moons by the time she was thirteen.

"I can smother a boy," Jane said giggling one night when they talked about being with boys and messing around. Cora could tell that Jane had already been sneaking off, maybe even with one of their brothers' friends, Cora thought, and almost gagged at the thought of it. She wasn't going to ask either. She just didn't want to know. But Jane said it was the Gibbs boy, and they'd meet each other a-way off in the woods toward the Gibbs's property that bordered the Ballard's. That side is rocky and full of bluffs. There's a creek back there and it's freezing cold down in those hollows. Jane told Cora that if you keep on going, there's an old cabin way back there, even has an old bed and a set-up like a little house, "like somebody done vanished into thin air who lived there," she said. "It had to be a woman," Jane whispered and looked around, even though all the boys were gone to the field. "Everything is decorated real feminine. There're even some nightgowns in a drawer of the dresser and dishes in the kitchen area, but just enough for two people. And, a vase with fake flowers on the dresser."

Cora gave her sister a worried look, thinking that maybe she was using her imagination a little too much so she could justify what she was doing out there with the Gibbs boy. Cora hoped that her sister hadn't been too eager and taken her freedom too far.

Cora was wishing she had Jane's breasts when Harold cleared his throat to get her attention again. Back to the most important question, "Why were you up at my house?" Cora asked suddenly. He took her hand and pulled her in close to him on the dance floor.

"I know your older brother," he said.

"Ben?"

He nodded. "I'm supposed to be around there tomorrow, so maybe I'll see you there," he said. Then, he pulled away and spun her around in a circle. He brought her in close to him again and asked, "Do you want to dance with me in the walk?"

Cora had made a lilac cake for the cake walk, and nobody else could replicate it. She wasn't going to tell anyone her secret ingredients, not for anything in the world. She wasn't going to deplete her storage of flower butter, and everything else she made from the flowers. She was saving up for her wedding cake. It had to be cool enough outside with low humidity, and the candied flowers couldn't get too hot. She used another trick for her coloring—berry stain from all types of plants, and some special ones that grew in the medicine wheel. Soaking certain berries in vinegar allowed her to generate dye. She made all types of different shades and colors to use for her cake and the decorations. Even to brighten the insides of a side pie and really make the cherries scorch your eyes with color. People smacked louder if the food looked a certain way. Hoot bragged, "Just too pretty to eat." She extended this to clothing and dyed some of the lace tablecloths she made into small lilac swirls for the side tables in the house.

Cora wouldn't have made the lilac cake for the festival, but Jane begged. Cora said, "Only a little one."

"But the magical way," Jane said, her hands clasped and squeezing her bosom, stretching the fabric of her dress to pull at the seams. Her eyes dreamily drifted toward the clouds. "With the magic ingredients?" she asked.

And Cora acquiesced, but just to a two-stack cake with the best ingredients. Cora thought that using some alcohol helps keep the food looking good.

The honey, whiskey and lemon balm mixture was a favorite of many people. Zona had a drink three nights a week. She liked to show that she could appreciate something and maintain her control—she said, "I don't have to keep on and on at something all the time, and that's more respectable."

On the dance floor at the Poke Sallet Festival, two dozen couples formed a line with their hands extended to the center—men on the right side, women on the left. The small band on the gymnasium stage began a big band swing tune, and the first couple began to follow the numbers and dance and twirl, being certain to hit all of the numbered squares on their way. Each couple followed behind and when someone missed a number or twisted and fell, they laughed and blushed, then strolled to the side to stand with the other spectators, who began to point, laugh, and even cheer. The Gibbs boy and Jane rocked forward, twirled, and turned, and Jane even flared her dress up and shook her breasts a little too much for the judges' approval. Their cousin Elizabeth was known to be quite a good dancer and she clapped her heels behind her back and even danced backward while hitting the numbers in the walk.

Cora got more nervous, thinking that she would ruin the dance for Harold by falling down or being too stiff. She couldn't think of any clever dance moves or any sneaky way to shake her body. Harold pulled her close and whispered, "I'll lead you, Cora. I like your body." She felt his chest press lightly against hers for an instant, as he took her hand behind her back and spun her over the first numbers, moving his body to the next, and rotating hers, holding her hips for another instant to guide, and then pausing with her in the moment. He looked at the audience, smiled, and gestured for the audience to clap without letting go of her hand. They clapped loudly to the beat. He turned with Cora and caught the momentum of the music between them, spinning her and grasping both of her hands until she flew down between his legs and back up again into the air to land on the final number. They danced until no one could keep up with their exuberance, and Harold chose Cora's lilac cake as his reward, while Jane sulked against the Gibbs boy's shoulder.

Harold ate dinner at their house the next evening. He brought the lilac cake back out to the house and Jane squealed with delight at the thought of eating it. She and the Gibbs boy had danced until her feet had blisters.

But at dinner, he didn't pay much attention to Cora at all. "Hello, Cora," he said when he arrived and went straight to delivering the cake to Zona and talking to Hoot and her brothers. They talked all through dinner, and, all the while, he just automatically thanked Hoot and Zona for dinner as if Cora wasn't the one dishing up everybody's plate and refilling their glasses. She even fried the poke sallet corn cakes, a special recipe that most folks didn't know, using the greens in a batter, and she added green onions just to make them perfect. He looked at Zona after the first bite and said, "They are something special, Zona," and she said, "Thank you," as if she had cooked them.

Finally, before leaving, he spoke to Cora, saying, "Good night. Thank you for a pleasant dinner," but that was the same thing he told Jane and everyone else, and then he, Ben, and Hoot took off on their horses with some loaded saddlebags. He had on a broad-rimmed cowboy hat, and Cora wanted to go away with him. She thought about going out for a ride by herself, and then stopped herself and went to do the dishes. Jane was eating the last crumbs of the lilac cake. "How'd you get another piece? You already ate Mama's piece," Cora scolded her. Jane looked wide-eyed between her shoulders, knowing that the real issue was that Cora had split a piece with Zona, in order to be polite, even though Zona was the only person anyone had ever heard tell of who didn't much care for lilac cakes. But Zona had asked from across the dinner table, "just give me half of yours, will you now, Cora?" So, she did.

And now, Jane was eating the half that Cora had given up. "I told her she could have my part," Zona said from her bedroom, the voice floating through the dark doorway and across the golden glow of the floorboards and into the kitchen, in front of the lamp, where Jane relaxed her shoulders, and held the last candied lilac flower on the tip of her finger, turning it in the light so that it sparkled. She giggled, placed it on her tongue, and closed her eyes in delight.

Zona had wanted a good daughter. Just one. And, Cora would be molded from the beginning into stifling her questions and her own imagination, her desires to do anything or to want to do anything on her own. As soon as she was born, Zona knew that Jane was not the good daughter. She was fighting away from her Mama from the beginning. She was sneaky and stole from the supplies of fruit and meat whenever possible. She took away from the hungry mouths and tired bodies of her brothers, but she never cared. She giggled. Jane also crafted ways to manipulate and get food from Cora on the side. People simply gave to Jane without worry for their own wants and desires. People—friends, relatives, even acquaintances—handed gifts and compliments, seats and spaces, to Jane without reservation, as if they'd already made a previous agreement. Their roles were a matter of fact.

Three days after the dinner, Harold was standing in front of their house with something in his hand, looking around nervously. It had already gone mid-morning. Cora walked out on the porch to get some fresh air, and he was standing there, peering down the road toward the fields. Cora hadn't even heard him come in. "How'd you get here?" she asked, looking for an automobile, but there wasn't one, and she heard his horse stamp and blow down at the little barn under the hill. They both laughed.

"I was going to talk to your brother and then, when I got here, realized they were all out today," he said.

"Yeah," Cora said. "So what can I do for you?"

"I wanted to give you this," he said. "And, I reckon I better go." He hesitated but handed her something heavy and wrapped in paper. "I'm supposed to come to dinner again tonight," he said. "I'll see you then."

She wondered why he was so awkward at her house, but he was so confident at the Poke Sallet Festival. Cora hung the horseshoe on the kitchen wall.

Zona said, "Where'd you get that?" as soon as she walked in from the fields.

"Harold brought it this morning," Cora said. It took about a half hour before what she said had sunk in to Zona's mind, as if it started to announce the future, something coming in the distance, like a thunderstorm on the land.

"Why'd he give you the pretty shoe?" Zona asked.

"I don't know," Cora said. "He just handed it to me and left." Harold continued to stop by the house for dinner and breakfast, until some people would think he was one of the brothers because he was with the family so much. He plucked the strings of the banjo with a dancing ease, up and down with march and movement, so quick and energetic. That summer, the only difference between Harold and the Ballard boys was that he turned in the direction of Colonel's barns and pastures, where he took care of Colonel's horses, the Tennessee Walkers, when the Ballard boys went out to tend the fields, care for the livestock, and make corn into shine. Colonel owned show horses, and Cora was mesmerized, like most people, to see the beautiful march as they pulled a carriage along the street—muscles surging with elegant power under the black coat. That's why Harold said he was at their house so much. He was training the horses to perfect their flat shod gait, looking after the horses, and speculating on selling or buying for Colonel. Harold wanted to stay in Kentucky where the Gentry's owned more stables and a riding school, a place where they not only had big lick beauties, naturally bred and trained to perform a gallant strut, but they also trained horses to run, he said, during dinner one night. He wanted to own some horses someday, and he was proud to work for honorable owners, who didn't use tricks and abuse their horses by soring.

"Even still, I wouldn't want to be someone's farrier forever or tend someone else's fields," he said, and then, smiled, "but I might forever sneak into the hollows to make shine," he laughed. The brothers rolled their eyes. He seemed more innocent than they, for some reason, but only in reference to what was supposed to be funny.

Cora knew he got his fair share of shine, and probably made a few deliveries, whether Hoot himself talked him into "doing a favor" or "earning a little extra," or some of Harold's own relatives or friends goaded him into bringing some shine back. Cora knew there was always more than the task claimed when her family had regular visitors.

The summer soaked that sun up into the fields, baked it like a butter pie, and drizzled it with wild berries and honey. Cora began to doubt any previous indications that Harold had eyes for her. He continued to make the same gestures with his eyes, his body, and even brought occasional small gifts, but these all became habitual, which almost made them seem bereft of admiration. She questioned his authenticity as well as her own ability to read other peoples' motives after weeks of the same behavior. The summer thunderheads swelled as thick as the cream and gathered frothy swirls of fat to please the tongue, and when the rains clamored down violently after making everything crackle with heat and desire for rain, the drops tasted sweeter to Cora's lips and mouth. However, she knew that the most pleasing of late summer tastes were the tart blackberries shielded by skin-tearing hooks that licked out at your bare flesh, as if it captured those little pricks of blood and sent them up the stem and into the berry seeds.

At dinner one night in late July, Cora talked to Jane across the table and said, so that Harold could hear, "I think the blackberries over up past the hot springs'll be ready to pick tomorrow, so I'm going over there to do that."

Zona loved blackberries and she begged for Cora to make it around to every patch on the property, wearing big old boots and carrying a gun to shoot any big rattlesnakes. Cora rode the horse, Giant, when she traveled across the property to gather berries of all sorts but especially mulberries, apples, and herbs that she collected from every spring's secret and wild field's edge. Giant was the easy rider, the gentlest of walkers, and Cora often let the children ride with her around the property. He was named Giant, but he was just a decent sized horse, maybe fifteen hands high, nothing massive, not like Ben's horse or Hoot's horse. They had about five big walkers and the rest were in the middle—spotted saddle horses on the smaller side. Giant was a chestnut color with black mane and tail and when he was young, he had a lovely canter and was used as a stud by Colonel a few times before he gave the horse to Hoot.

Harold was already at the blackberry hedge when Cora and Giant approached over the slope of the hill. His horse was tied off under a tree, and he wiped the sweat from his neck and forehead, having already gathered a bushel of berries before Cora got there. "Heard you say that you were riding out here this morning, so I invited myself," he said. "I hope you don't mind. You can take these back with you."

"I think you're teasing me, Harold," Cora said without getting down from Giant who tried to turn around, but Cora made him turn back again. Cora was angry, and the sources were the late, festering summer heat and irritation from Harold's partial romantic interest.

He laughed, and when she turned to go away for good, he shouted. "I apologize, Cora!" he said. "I'm not teasing. That's a promise." He waited when she paused, but she continued on a few steps when he didn't say anything. "I like you!" he shouted again and ran toward her. "Wait."

When he reached her, he took the reins of the horse. She refused his hand when she dismounted, but he quickly tied Giant beside his horse. He stood under the tree, watching Cora gather blackberries without speaking to him.

Harold brushed his arm against Cora and got himself tangled so that she was forced to help him out of the briars—anything to signal his interest. Anyone else would've known what he was getting at. Cora wasn't sure anymore. She was confused by him, her own feelings, maturity, and why he would show up unannounced. She was so frazzled under the surface.

The junebugs hid in the brambles and rattled their bodies, vibrating the berries and startling Harold. "Ah!" He screamed and almost fell backward, "Damn junebug! Thought it was a rattler," he said. He was so electrified by then, trading energies with Cora that he tripped on a briar again, and she giggled in spite of her reluctance to trust. She thought he was rather agile usually, but he seemed almost clumsy that morning. Suddenly, he leapt forward with a kiss—a complete surprise, and she dropped her blackberries and felt as if her mouth were paralyzed, frozen solid, but his was like a big, wet blackberry tasting her mouth, gently biting at her lip and giving it tender touches and licks. She didn't dare move, even if she was charged from her toes to her scalp, and thought she'd jump right out of her skin, thought her skin would pulse from every vein, through every pore. Finally, her toes wiggled back and forth in her boots, her chest trembled, and she giggled again.

The junebugs rattled the briars again and this time *she* jumped, but in the direction she hadn't intended, straight into his body. His hand moved to her waist and started to feel along her waistline, as she smiled during his kisses on her mouth. She continued to laugh and to shake more and more, until finally pushing him away once she was suddenly aware of the heaviness of his presence. She grabbed his wrist with her other hand and he laughed, paused, and she dropped his arm, suddenly aware. He reached out his other hand and touched her face. "You okay?" he asked. She couldn't stop laughing.

He arched an eyebrow, "Have you ever kissed anyone before?"

She was silent, blushed quickly, and bent to pick up the fallen blackberries. She wanted to cry because she was imagining that he kissed plenty of girls, more like women, and she felt so simple and plain.

"Do you want to do it again?" he asked. "Or, was I really bad at it and that's why you're laughing?"

Her smile invited him to kiss her again, and this time, she wasn't as shy and after a few minutes, she pushed him down in front of the blackberries, where they met the honeysuckle vine and the shady edge of the forest. Then, it was he who couldn't stop laughing, and he held her there, sweating and lying on top of him. She didn't want to move. It was perfect. He cradled her small body and they stayed like that until they almost fell asleep, but the crickets stirred, and they kissed for a long time. Her lips ached. She couldn't remember what finally made them

SHANA THORNTON

stop kissing. Harold helped her onto her horse and then left in a different direction once the sun passed overhead, saying he would meet her again in a few days.

Cora went two days in a row to the hot spring in the evening so that no one would suspect anything. She didn't think they would anyway. She was so hurried by her naïve pleasure that she considered nothing else, no one else. She wasn't thinking far outside of the moment in any situation. The spring was well hidden and canopied, and they always burned sage and cedar to make the mosquitoes stay away. She was wearing her bathing dress and Harold just took his shorts right off in the water after he'd been kissing her for a little while. He felt inside of her dress and held her breasts in his hands. She flinched and made a motion to go under water because he had pushed her back on a rock that was like a chair and her breasts were above the water. But he said, "Please, don't. May I just look at them?" Her toes wiggled under water and her nipples hardened above the warm water. But, he didn't just look, he gawked, and then she couldn't stop herself from getting into the water and pressing against him. She pressed and moved and wiggled, and it was all so fluid and warm, just perfect for young lovers. She knew it felt good but she didn't know any more than that.

She met him there through the end of summer, and then he had to go back up to Kentucky. He wrote her letters and they were nice, but he knew her parents or brothers or somebody would read them and he was smart enough to know that "befriending" her wouldn't last long. A letter arrived announcing that he was taking a position

86

as an apprentice to a farrier in England, "a real dream come true," he wrote, but he hadn't ever mentioned anything like that to Cora. He promised to "keep writing, and maybe we'll see each other again someday."

She burned the letter. She walked straight out to the medicine wheel and set it on fire and let the words scorch blue, red, orange, yellow, gray, black, white, gray again and float away on the wind. Ashes. Dust. In a daze, Cora prepared the dinner in the new Sears and Roebuck house, the one with the new beginning and promise, where she had thought about Harold for every meal and made the food he ate and listened and laughed and welcomed and embraced him. Cora searched through the tasks she performed, but it was all foggy and she couldn't understand where her life was going to go. Zona stared at her daughter for a long time, seeing if she could maintain eye contact for as long as she wanted to look, through dinner and over the dishes. Cora kept up her trips to the hot spring even after Harold left. Cora thought he would come back for the holidays and talk to her father about marriage.

She wrote to Harold and told him stories about her brothers and said she learned to become a better gossip around the town, and when she went to the market, she stopped in the drugstore and made some excuse to look around and eavesdrop. She asked her brothers to tell whatever gossip they may have heard from their friends so that he would have something interesting to read. Plus, she just figured that her Mama was reading the letters anyway, so she better stick to everybody else and not herself.

SHANA THORNTON

She wanted to tell Harold that she always planned to make a big lilac cake for her wedding, and that she saved pearls and stones for a dress that she wanted to embroider. That she imagined lilac and rose blooms in her hair. That she didn't care if they had to live in Kentucky, or England, but she wanted to go with him. She put them in every possible picture—their own house, decorating, and building a fire. She could smoke a cigarette every night if she wanted to and if they lived in town somewhere, she could have hot water in a bath on the house. She was thinking about a baby in a crib, and watching them grow up, because they would have more than one, and how the children would look like both of them. She had never been to the ocean but she could see them on the shoreline—five of them, smiling, the little one playing in the sand, a baby on her hip and Harold with his arm around her waist. They were a good lookin' family, Cora thought.

And, just like that, Jane was finished playing pretend with the Gibbs boy in the cabin. She was getting married for real. Gibbs—that's what the Ballard family just kept on calling him—inherited his granddaddy's farm in Davidson County. Gibbs was in love with Jane, so he didn't want to go to the new farm without her. He had come over and asked Hoot's permission, displaying the ring. Hoot said, "Of course you can't go without Jane. That's a smart decision." Just as smart as Zona's offering that she and Cora would make all of the food for the wedding, including the lilac cake, but the flowers weren't in season so it could never be as beautiful as the one Cora was saving for her wedding to Harold.

****

When a storm came across the landscape, Cora knew it was from a place she had never visited. The ocean. The clouds and sky looked like pictures of the ocean she had seen in the National Geographic magazines she saw at Jane's house. After Jane got married, Cora made three trips to her sister's new farm, and they went up to Nashville a few times.

An approaching thunderhead transformed into waves of clouds and smelled like she imagined the ocean smelled all the time, like after a fertile rain. Cora wished herself away from that land so many times, wished it was all gone and didn't matter. She began to lose appreciation and fumbled for it in the kitchen, where you could see the changes and know your part mattered.

Her brother John was in the war later, and he said the ocean smelled like the stinkiest bucket of fish you ever caught and left for a few days out by the river. She preferred her picture of rain and water. What was the smell of water anyway? She wondered. Did it change with whatever was near it? She thought it did. Maybe water smell was the fish. All life was watery.

She cooked fish every day that the moon was in Pisces. That was the only constant, something she started in order to satisfy nature in herself. Make magic flow through the blood, the body. That's how her special recipes began, and she thinks Nenny was the one to sprinkle those first inklings of food magic into Cora's fingers. More than fingers and flourish, preparing food was solid, wrist action, forearm motions, arms with hold and heft and space enough to tilt in and out of ovens and countertops, the push of grinding the pestle into mortar, the crush and twist of plant life, the splinter and crackle of bone and ligament, the suction of feather and muscle from animal life, the squeeze and tug of teats for milk, splashing water and milk and whiskey, sticking the honey, the dough, the meal, the grind of grains, the pummeling and molding to make taste.

Cora's grandma, Nenny, planted the sunroot in the medicine wheel with Cora, and Jane charged in with her own spade, determined to know what was so special. The sunroot collected nutrients all year long, and after the harvest and fullness of Christmas, the New Year always needed something special.

While Cora and Jane both planted the sunroot, Cora was the one to bundle herself in hides and wool during January and chop at the hard, cold earth to get the roots, to pry those tubers loose from the winter chill. She peeled them and plopped the cubes in a buttered iron skillet for ten minutes. She made the sauce for them from milk and the heavy fresh cream from her favorite milk cow and added flour and butter, thyme, and grated nutmeg. She baked them in a covered pottery dish in the brick oven.

Years later, when she was an old woman, this recipe was one Aunt Cora gave to me, saying, "The sunroot is really what folks call the Jerusalem artichoke." She laughed. "Not an artichoke at all. Some plants need to claim the likeness of another one to survive, I guess."

Nenny taught Cora about the pigweed, called amaranthus. She followed Nenny in late May and early June to collect the young leaves. They filled jars with the shiny black seeds, parched them in boiling water, and ground them with a tall pestle into meal. Later, Cora baked small semi-savory cakes that she poured honey over.

Nenny showed her how to satisfy others with the old flavors, as she called them, "the original ones to this, our homeland." The sacred combination began with the three sisters—beans, corn, and squash sent from the harvest mother, and it was said that Nenny insisted on planting a small section of the three on the side of every garden plot. Beans, corn, and squash. Nenny insisted that purple hull peas, purple carrots, and tomatoes were their cousins—the other three sisters. Fried large squash flowers and whole squash baked in a fire pit were also delicacies handed down from Nenny.

The tricks and secrets were Nenny's magic, but she never intended for them to be misused or abused. The turkey mullein and vinegar weed made the fish dumb, and Cora could grab right into the river from the gravel bar and grasp with her hands if she wanted to, but mostly, she used a net, except for the time she wanted to impress Harold. He didn't understand what it meant to "smell the fish" or how to fish at night, much less how to feed them what they like.

Cora cultivated the cattails growing in the river run offs and made flour from the pollen. She waited for the pollen heads to swell and soften and then she made a loaf of bread, but she loved to dig the roots and make soups.

Often, digging roots brought out more treats than any other parts of the plants. The sweet-flag candy brought joy from her own ground instead of paying someone behind a counter at the five-and-dime.

Cora would always return to the kitchen, the stove, the hot coals, the pantry spices, the lids and labels, the canning cellar, the root crops dank and sleeping, the empty jars sweating while waiting—oh, how they yearn for fillings and flavors. She would fill it—the need, the desire for satisfaction and satiety at once.

"The talent to cook brings people together," Hoot said. "You don't have to compete, little Cora. You are sustaining life all the time."

****

The humidity, everyone said, was worse than the heat, yet Cora noticed how they all ran inside or to the shade or the river, even when it was only hot and there wasn't a mosquito's percentage of humidity.

She walked in a puddle of sweat, rode in a hot car with windows rolled down in July and August. Her dress was imprinted with her butt cheeks' slippery efforts at sitting in the seat. She slept in the middle of a freshly bush-hogged field. Her skin electrified and softened into earthy brown after an hour of being inside again.

"I can't sleep in this heat," Zona said, when she came upon Cora lying in a field one afternoon. Zona's shadow blocked the light. "Why do you punish yourself just to be alone?" Zona asked over her shoulder as she continued on toward the house.

Later, Cora percolated black coffee on the stove for lunch. Was there a boiling point for Cora? She reclined against the hot roof of the well house and allowed the heat to soak through her dress, through to her bones. Her feet rested on the stone well wall. She wondered if it would literally cook her. A seared back, she imagined, and cringed at the thought. She eased her back away from the roof and sat on the well wall, her legs hanging off, toes falling away to either side as she faced the sun. She rested there until she felt herself glowing from the sun, and then she went inside and cooked. She could see the sun and soil in the vegetable skins and the exuberance of life in their fleshy pockets, the exultation of soaking in light energy. She held their star heat in her hands, sliced into it, and transformed it again with the energy she had been given.

"What's gotten into you?" they all asked.

****

"Don't tell that story," Zona said to Cora's grandmother, whom they called "Nenny." Even if Cora hadn't been paying attention to either of them before that, she perked up and wanted to know a secret.

But Nenny was so old by then that she didn't care anymore what Zona or anyone else said, and just told the story, "Oh, needs to be told. A Shawnee girl, probably just a young girl, about fourteen, watched from the banks. Said her people were the ones bedded down here originally. They built little cabins along the river runoffs, along the streams and creeks. They were smart people, farming not much different than us, and using those caves to store their meat and preserve. They used everything—the river to fish, for mussels, too, mmmMMMmm, yes, baby girl, and sucking out the pennywinkle meat that we don't have no more, all gone from too many people and contamination. Probably, all those riverboats. Her village used that cold spring from the cave to get good water. And, they made a fort not far from here, so the Shawnee controlled the river traffic and kept a watch on the long hunters, trading with them." Nenny leaned forward onto her elbows and rolled tobacco between a cigarette paper. "The French men wanted Nashville with a yearning, that's what they say. Called it French Lick, but that didn't last long once the military cut the wagon road through—the Avery Trace came a little later."

She licked the cigarette paper quickly and rolled it shut in one motion, and struck a match. The fire flared when the match flame touched the loose paper and tobacco that dangled from the end. She closed her eyes for a moment and leaned back again. She spoke as she exhaled. "The French explored from Canada and connected to the Mississippi River, then crossed over and reached the point to trade with the Shawnee. He was a coureur des bois, woods runner, they called them. Those men were trying to find out about this wilderness, and they toughened themselves against the cold winter bitterness and the fire heat of summer. They fought cougar and wolf. They hunted buffalo, not just deer."

Nenny winked at the young Cora and continued smoking intense draws from the cigarette. "The Shawnee girl spied on him, one of the hunters. He didn't suspect her, didn't spy her anywhere. Finally, she planned it and showed herself to him like the Mother Earth. They rolled in the meadows and ran the forests. They danced across the hills on the backs of the horses. He brought his horse. She had a brown mare, only gentle with her, like a dog who comes and goes; her horse spent a night in the meadow and then in the Shawnee village and in the forest on another night. They leapt along the river forks and found untamed places of green and sparkling enchantment as the plants and flowers, the water and dragonflies glided down the creeks. She fed corn, melons, and squash to the hunter. She boiled the mussels until they opened their delicacies to him. He must have been surprised at her pottery, and her tools and weapons. She cooked in a big oven by the river and made bowls. I have one here. That's how Colonel's Ma told it. This...," Nenny stood and crossed the cabin, tapped into a crooked, old, brown bowl with thick clay and some cracks. "Still holds water, even with cracks," Nenny said and returned to her seat with the cigarette smoke trailing behind.

"Come here," she said to Cora. When Cora stood in front of her, Nenny reached a knobby, creased hand up to her. Cora didn't know what Nenny was about to put in her hand, and then she felt cool, smooth pieces in her palm. She turned the seeds over with her fingertips. They looked like those from a melon, some colorful corn kernels, and different types of dried beans.

Nenny continued, "Colonel's Ma says they called her Little Flowering Plant, and the hunter was called Woods Runner by the family. This French Woods Runner had been trading all along the traces, hunting pelts, but his fortune was stuck together with honey so the coins wouldn't jangle against one another, and he wrapped them in stained old cloth, so they wouldn't announce the wealth he was slowly accumulating so that he could run away and buy lands out west that they thought would be owned by France. The French and Indian War pushed the French out, and those men like him, the coureurs de bois, would suffer the most. They were outlaws from all sides. The king wanted to tax the hides they had hunted in a land claimed by too many people. They could hardly make it back alive to sell the pelts. Woods Runner would have been a hard man. But Little Flowering Plant would have been a difficult woman, just the same. Reminiscent of bind weed, stinging nettles, wild rose thorns, blackberry hooks," Nenny chuckled, paused, and closed her eyes. Cora thought the story was finished.

"What happened to them?" Cora asked.

Nenny opened her eyes and took another draw from the cigarette. "Woods Runner was lucky to have her tribe as his family," Nenny said. "They allowed him to leave and return again and again, season after season and year after year, even when they had a baby together, that's what

Colonel's Ma told me. Colonel's family, your Papa's family, has one of the original homesteads in this county. Fulton Ballard was a Navy captain, took some acres for his service, about two hundred and fifty, they say, on the river and operated an inn and a store for settlers traveling along the road. There was nothing else for a long time. One of his sons fought with Andrew Jackson, and he made a little money from his battles and speculations, investments; seems he was a lawyer, Justice of the Peace and whatnot. He liked the looks of this place and bought it, some two hundred and fifty acres to match his father." She stopped and reclined, closing her eyes again, the cigarette finally burning down to the smaller end with its heavily streaked and darkened, oily bronze end. She had fresh tobacco stain on her lips. "He married the child of Little Flowering Plant and Woods Runner. Colonel's Ma told it that way to me, and I say it's the Gospel truth. Remember this, Cora." Nenny opened her eyes, dropped the cigarette into a spittoon next to her chair. "Woods Runner always followed the river to the place where it created a horse's hoof, north of the fort at Granville."

"Pttah!" Zona mouthed and tried to interrupt, waving a hand in front of her face as if Nenny was full of nonsense.

But Nenny just spoke louder and faster, "Her village got the scarlet fever is what everybody thinks. That's what happened to most of them Shawnee villages along the river, but probably after Woods Runner disappeared. Colonel's Ma said that it was told that he just disappeared, didn't come back, and I expect he died in the wilderness or trying to get back to it. We won't ever know because the story is just told and told down the generations."

Zona was sighing and grunting, stomping her feet at whatever chore she was pretending to do.

Nenny waved her arm and leaned in closer to Cora, to the very tip of the chair, "*and some people* try to say it's not true, but it *is* the Gospel truth."

Young Cora looked surprised. She was beginning to put it all together because she knew their part of the river looked like a horse's hoof and just south it flows into the shape of a horse's head, if you look at a map, even to this day. Cora had been hearing hints about some secret gold coins all her life and never realizing it might be real. She always thought it was a joke and as Nenny was telling the story all the way, Cora knew it wasn't just a bunch of giggling about there being "gold coins buried somewhere on the property, left by an Indian and some kind of a wild French runner."

"Crazier'n Hell," Cora's brothers always laughed behind Nenny's back when their grandmother said anything about gold or coins or buried things on the property. It was a joke that she was just crazy and made up stories. Zona never let Cora hear the whole story, until then.

Zona's explanation to Cora was, "The settlers made up stories to entertain themselves. This one got passed down."

"Shouldn't somebody try to find the gold?" Cora asked her Mama.

Zona laughed. "Don't you think just about every one of them has tried to find it and act like he's not looking for it? They think that we don't notice random holes all over the property. Sometimes, they get too lazy or frustrated to fill them back in."

"Is that what those holes are for over by the Fulton Hill?"

Zona laughed so hard she almost fell over. "Those boys. They make fun of Nenny but she's got them out there digging all over the hills. Even your Daddy tried to find it for awhile. She's convincing. I think she really believes it by now, she's been telling it so long."

"Did she make it up?" Cora asked

"No, your father's grandma did tell it," Zona said.

"Where did she hear it from?"

"Like Nenny said, 'passed down the generations,'" Zona said.

Later, Cora asked Nenny, and she said, "It was the family's story. Real Shawnee story."

****

"That would have been Colonel's great-great-great grandma who survived the fever and married the lawyer son of Captain Fulton," Aunt Cora said to me when she finished telling me the story.

"Do you think it was true?" I asked Aunt Cora.

"Oh yeah, honey, oh yeah," she said. "And I'd like to see the treasure. More than gold coins in that stash, you can count your chickens."

"Well, where do you think it is?" I asked

"Lord ah mighty, good God," she sighed. "Buried out there somewhere."

"Weren't there any clues in the story about where they buried this treasure?" I asked.

"I guess it was the horse's hoof and that was it. The property connected to the horse's hoof," she said. "That's the only clue."

I bought a metal detector on my way home and looked at the calendar. When could I go out there and look around? Maybe I could get lucky. Miss Emy still lived in the old Sears and Roebuck home on twenty-five acres of land that stretched back to the river. She sold the rest when my Dad needed the money for drugs, rehab, and paying for his head, and I mean keeping it attached to his body, so that the dealers didn't kill him. It's a real thing—that someone can bet the Devil his head.

****

Aunt Cora came from a time of letters, when you had to consider someone's words, when a response took time to compose and wasn't an immediate response, a knee jerk reaction in a text message or a tweet or a Facebook comment. Rarely could a letter be received, read, and then a response written and posted and sent out in the same day. Yes—a letter was all about time. Savoring the written word, considering, enjoying, and sharing in a letter of your own. If a dispute arose, it was generally about a major event or trespass, not a trivial issue, for time, energy, and resources were too valuable to waste on anything as trivial as simple likes and dislikes about personal activities and household chores. Life was household chores. Nothing was convenient, not even communication so there was little time for petty disputes.

I wish it was still that way, but seems like my friends are always wrapped up in a Facebook dispute about whether or not someone actually deleted a friend's post or failed to like it. Aunt Cora has no idea what Facebook is. She has a vague idea about computers that has never developed beyond seeing them as contemporary typewriters. I stopped trying to explain it. She always waves me over to her chair as soon as I arrive at Melinda's house to visit. "Oh, good, Robin, come here, please make this thing work." She hands me the remote control or points to the record player. She wants the sound to come from the speakers on the entertainment center, so I plug in the cables correctly, and we hear Koko Taylor all of a sudden. I must look shocked because she laughs in big cackles as I would imagine Koko herself laughing. My eyes must have grown even bigger because she can't stop the big belly laughter bellowing out of her ninety-year-old body. She always had a large mouth, one of those stretchy smiles, and it has taken over in the moment. I almost fall over from the giggles at imagining her "pitching a wang dang doodle all night long" in her youth, right behind her Mama's backside, and I realize that I don't even know the half of it, and she's never going to tell me unless I bring her some whiskey in the future.

After the song finished, she motioned for me to turn the dial down on the speakers so we could talk along with the music. I asked her about the letters from the farrier. I knew his name was Harold, but I liked to call him "the farrier." This made Cora laugh. "Must be the writer in you," Cora said. "Making it more official, like some kind of a title instead of an occupation."

She stared out the window at the daylilies planted along the front sidewalk.

"There weren't many letters," Cora continued after a moment. "He described what it was like to cross the ocean, and he went by boat, honey, took a long time to get over there, and to finally settle down, took him even more time. It felt like the whole year had passed, but it was just about six months before I got that first letter. The last one I got was between Christmas and New Year's Day. I don't know if he sent any more and I didn't get them, but I never did see another one the following spring and I was looking with longing and kept looking. I don't think my heart stopped hoping I'd open the mailbox and find my name written with his hand until I married and moved away from there. It was like the mailbox could never be the same again."

****

When she was by the brick oven in the old house, Cora felt the fire flame on her face, circling it, cupping her cheeks with its fire-hands, fingers flickering on her brow. The farrier knew heat the same as Cora, knew transformation and chemistry, how a flame can do what is pure—fierce beauty—and you better be afraid and amused by its wildness.

Cora's horse, Giant, her boy, could ride in heat when most other horses had to cool down. He seemed engorged with energy, pulsing in his canter around the fields, begging for the shade of the forest. For moving under the trees in the soft, warm patches of mud and leaves.

Cora stopped her fluid recollections about the farrier and the horses.

****

Aunt Cora looked solid, but her wrinkles made the edges of her face stack up like a limestone bluff in little brown streaked sheets. She stared at me with that hard face, no softening, "Mama done me wrong," she said. "She kept me there. I didn't marry until I was nearly forty. All I did was care for the babies, cook, and clean. I loved Paul, couldn't leave him, my baby. He was like *my* baby. I was seventeen when he was born."

"You mean you didn't marry the farrier later?" I asked.

"No, honey, I never heard from him again," Aunt Cora said.

CHAPTER 4

ASSIGNMENT FOUR

Melinda, 1980s & '90s

I was avoiding the first decision I made with the class—to find my Dad, who was homeless, but clean—meaning that he was not using drugs and hadn't been using for a while. The last time Miss Emy saw him was three months before my class began. When he had some money from selling *The Patron*, a Nashville street paper, he called her from his cell phone because he could pay to add minutes. Selling the paper allowed him to share rent and bills with other men in a shelter that provided low-income housing to former addicts with jobs. People assume that everyone who sells *The Patron* is homeless, and some won't buy a paper if they notice that he has a cell phone or is wearing a decent shirt and pants. They don't consider that some homeless people have families who do try to help them. I bought the cell phone when I was seventeen, as a gift for my Dad after he got out of rehab. I paid for 500 minutes to begin, so that he had a phone for jobs and to keep in touch. That was his fourth time in rehab.

When I considered finding him, even if he was in an apartment and selling the paper, I dreaded the encounter in case he needed money. I didn't want to tell him exactly where I was living, even though I knew he could find my apartment, and may show up on my university campus someday if he was desperate enough. But, all of those ideas were fears, because Miss Emy was his primary patron.

Miss Emy's two daughters were my aunts—Carolyn and Melinda. Miss Emy always said that Melinda loved nothing more than to pry into other peoples' stories. Miss Emy shook her head and rolled her hands over themselves, as if she were smoothing her fingers, a nervous habit that increased as she aged if she didn't have a fan to flutter. She smiled, looking into her open fingers, and said, "Melinda was the worst of them all—all the gossips I've ever known, but she could smell a lie quicker than anybody else I ever knew, too." She smoothed her fingers again and looked at me, making sure I was getting the story straight if I was going to tell it. She told me more than once, "I guess if you're going to tell it, you better do it right."

Miss Emy always worried about Daniel, my Dad. He was her baby boy, hanging on her legs and skirt hem since he could pull himself up from a crawl, crying for her to hold him. She always said that's when things started to really go wrong in her marriage with Paul, my grandpa. He always wanted a son so badly and, then, here was this boy always begging for his Mama. And he was a Mama's boy, but Paul didn't like it and tried to teach him, wanting the baby to be a tiny man before he was even out of diapers. With a son, Paul became a different father, a different man—loaded with expectations.

And, there she was—Melinda—in the middle of everything, provoking her Dad so that she could become the favorite, snickering and laughing at her brother Daniel, the little baby "Mama's boy," pointing her know-it-all finger, constantly causing trouble. Melinda owned the confidence of their father, even and especially when he was wrong. "It's as if they said something enough, it would be true," Miss Emy said. "She knew how to play with her little giggles and head tucked between her brown shoulders. She was always fond of any little bit of attention. She found ways to start some cute meanness with her siblings, and then she'd go back and love on them to win them over again. Always, drama. And she took special delight in tormenting Daniel," Miss Emy said.

I could imagine that Melinda's playfulness tiptoed with bursts of fairy laughter and her brown eyes gleamed in mischievous plans with earth and dung and other farm elements. Pranks came naturally, as once she hitched her brother to a rope and pulley by the belt loop and strung him from the peak of the barn so that he flew out in wild shouts over the ground until he met it with a thud when the threads of the belt loop broke. She also dared him to taunt the bull in the pasture and run across the field, while she watched from behind the fence. He still tells the story about the breath of the bull and the shock of the electric fence on the crown of his head when he scooted under it.

Sometimes, he jokes and it sounds like a statement, but most of the time he says, "She was out to kill me, I believe?" as a question when the pranks come up in conversation. When they went to the house in Nashville for the weekend, she convinced him to be her hero and try to burn a mouse out of its hole, and he caught the kitchen on fire. The pranks went on until he became wise to her manipulations, but then he was in the company of the men, his father and his father's brothers, and my Dad would learn how real manipulation can electrify.

Dad didn't say a lot about how he got started on heroin. When Miss Emy found some traces of it and wasn't sure what it was, my aunt Melinda identified it— the actual drugs in our house.

I wanted to know who introduced my Dad to heroin in the first place. That was one of the main answers I wanted, and maybe that's strange, but I think the source of something that problematic and engaging at the same time should give me insight into my Dad's addiction. That answer came as one of the easiest in the end. Of course, I grew up with my Dad being checked out, and, when he did talk, spouting stories that tangled me up in chasing my own tail, even if he didn't know what I was after with all my questions. He always thought I wanted to be a "know-it-all, just like your Aunt Melinda." He liked to say that, as a diversion.

He needed diversions for what he had done. In its worst state, the farm was a mess. Within ten years, Hoot, Zona, and Paul died, and all from disease and natural causes. Hoot and Paul both suffered strokes and went downhill suddenly, while Zona did not even attempt to seek treatment for the cancer diagnosis she was given, or she may have lived much longer. Miss Emy was lost without them, and the extended family was scattered, busy with their own lives. Daniel was the only child left living on the farm, and he was twenty, working in a local mine and devastated with the sudden change in their way of life. He was to step up and run the farm for Miss Emy, that's what she expected, so he found an eighteen-year-old wife from the trailer park, and the two of them eloped. He moved Miss Emy into Hoot and Zona's big farmhouse and himself and his wife into the home where he was born.

My aunt Melinda said of my Mama, "She was just a little pretty thing who wanted to be rescued." In the next year, I was born, and Mama died in a car wreck not long after that. "It was so sad," Melinda said. "I felt so sorry for him. Poor Daniel, he had a lot of bad luck, and I guess that's why we've always tried to help him. We felt sorry for him. But I had to stop feeling guilty and responsible for him. He stole money, my car stereo one time, even my whiskey." She arched an eyebrow. "You might as well know what he's like so you can protect yourself since you're becoming an adult now." She hugged me and patted my back with those swift stinging taps. She enjoys hugs—the ones that squeeze me—and pinching my cheeks if she feels like it, and "spanking your rear end;" she'll laugh and actually do it, but she holds my hand, too, and treats me like a daughter most of the time.

During its bad times, the farmhouse contained crumbs embedded in the carpet. For the little time I lived with my Dad in the house where he and his sisters were born, there was a soured smell emanating from the sink. Cigarette clouds floated through the house, even when he wasn't there. I huddled over an old iron stove in the wintertime, and I liked to put my blanket on the top of it before I went to bed so that it was warm in my drafty room. In the kitchen, a thin, dirty dishrag lay in a shallow puddle of cloudy water, and often there were a few pieces of soggy noodles, swelled to capacity. Limp cigarette butts floated around with the remaining tobacco shredded and stuck to the side of the sink. A pot with a crust of gravy from yesterday buzzed with gnats next to a pot crusted with pinto beans. Sliced tomatoes were partially shriveled and dried, and flies infested their open saucer. There'd be a pile of slop in a plastic bowl, ready to go out to the hogs. The place was fecund even in the winter. Shag carpet was in the bedroom that my Dad never wanted to drag the canister vacuum around to clean. Outside, the air was loaded with mooing, bleating, cooing, barking, crowing, roosting, snorting, and squealing of animals. Cow pastures backed up to the house.

I was uncomfortable if it was quiet—always worried, thinking that it was about time for my Dad to show up and start yelling at me or somebody he wished he could talk to, as if he were talking to *them*, raging on and on about how someone was unfair to him or cheated him out of some money, even though he was so deep in his addictive need that we didn't know if he was telling the truth or not.

I wanted to drown him out, forget, escape…without annoying or startling him. When I played my old guitar, left over from the family meeting days, he left me alone. He confessed that it could soothe his soul sometimes. I tried to pluck the mandolin and the violin, even an old banjo, or pound out a rhythm on the hand drums, rattle the sticks, and all that old stuff, not knowing their stories. I liked the guitar best, so I wore my fingertips out.

When it was quiet, I tried to listen and enjoy it, but wondered where all the animals went. What was going on? Something needed to crow, so I didn't have to worry about my Dad. The stillness silenced even the crickets rubbing their legs together, and I imagined making sounds like the animals and insects, rubbing the strings across my fingers, making a vibration in my throat to hum…imitating songs I heard. I always got disrupted by something. A roach might run quickly across the floor and make me scream.

"That's a water bug," Miss Emy would inform me if she came to clean the house. She scrubbed the tub with powder sprinkles and hot water. She set off the bug bombs the next day.

"Let's go," she said after covering the dishes in the dish drain with a towel. "Put some paper towels over those, right there," she said pointing to some glasses sitting on the counter close to me.

"Shouldn't we use more than a napkin?" I asked.

111

"I bought Bounty at the store yesterday. They're the good ones," she reassured me.

Everything about the ordeal became predictable. We did it every two or three months. We moved slowly out of the gravel driveway next to the house, and then she jerked us to a stop, suddenly slamming the lever into park and then into reverse. "Shit!" she said. "I left a pack of cigarettes in there. Honey, run in there and grab his cigarettes. I don't want that bug bomb stuff on them. Here," she said after swiftly backing up close to the door, "you'll need the keys. Hurry up! And don't breathe it in," she said. As I opened the door, I heard her yelling, "Robin," she shouted through the window, "There's a carton. Grab the whole carton on top of the refrigerator!"

My Dad's older sister, Carolyn, sold cleaning products then, and later, makeup and always hosted makeup parties. She and her husband lived about three hours away toward Knoxville with a bunch of kids, four, and were constantly swapping children with her husband's relatives and taking family vacations together with them.

Aunt Melinda moved back to Nashville and into one of the rooms in the house there while my grandpa was alive, and after he died, she bought the Nashville house from Miss Emy. She sold ads for *The Nashville Banner* until she found her way onto one of the radio programs and then, a television morning show. "She became a career woman," Miss Emy would say. Her show was called *Music City Mornings* with Melinda Ballard, and I woke up early to watch her. I wanted everyone to know that she was my aunt. Over the years, she had three different co-hosts, one with two first names like Roger Brent, and another whose complete name I can't remember because every time he said it, he made a weird pointing finger motion with both hands, "Sebastian Something" and finally, the singer who tried to sing all of his lines and only lasted two mornings. The producers finally decided to ditch the co-hosts and it has always been the channel 6, *Music City Mornings* with Melinda Ballard, beginning at 5 a.m. They have guest hosts and celebrities, mostly singers, who make cameos. She's proud of her ratings and everywhere she goes in middle Tennessee, people whisper, "Oh, I know her." The old timers are especially fond of her since they wake up early.

She was always nice enough to give me her hand-me-down clothes. She went to junk stores off Charlotte Avenue and bought boxes of clothes from Spiegel and Castner-Knott. In the '80s, her dresses were covered in lace, vest attachments, ties, ribbon pulls, zippers, and it was like getting strapped into a ride just to try on the clothes she found. You might find yourself rubbed raw in places that you didn't know it was possible for clothes to reach. Melinda owned stirrup pants that looped your third toe and arched up to a necktie. Your chakras would be aligned, and she could tell you how to do it. She outfitted me once in a silk wrap-around skirt and puffy-sleeved shirt. Those shoulder pads were bigger than my face.

Around that same time, Melinda showed up at Thanksgiving dinner wearing a necktie, suspenders with her pants, and stiletto heels. My Dad made such fun of her by singing like Boy George and calling her "Karma

Melinda" to the tune of "Karma Chameleon" that she went into a rage and flung potatoes au gratin at him across the table. Of course, they were hot and that made him furious. Then he lunged at her and knocked the table against the wall, and food covered all of us who were sitting on that side. Melinda had evaded his threats and laughed at the spectacle, and that only made it all worse. He cussed everyone and chased Melinda into the front yard. She ran right out of her stilettos and into her red car, the Firebird that made us all jealous of her. I was so glad that Miss Emy hid the keys to the truck and acted like my Dad lost them, so that he couldn't chase Melinda into town and cause a big scene while he was in withdrawals from being high. We all knew he had been shooting up again, just by the jittery way he acted and the fact that he kept making up some story for why he needed more money from Miss Emy.

He drove Hoot's old, beat-up truck. Carolyn had a brown Ford station wagon. Strangely enough, Miss Emy no longer owned a Ford after my grandpa died. She drove an Oldsmobile. She'd say, "Open the glove box, Robin, and give me a fan. It's too hot out here today. Get you one if you're hot." I handed Miss Emy a fan printed by the church with a long-haired, hippie-looking image of Christ wearing a cream-colored robe and sandals walking along a fertile desert scene. My other choices were fans printed by politicians for local elections with messages like "Vote Ben 'Buddy' Anderson for Superintendent', or fans printed by funeral homes and nursing homes with photographs of the buildings, a Bible, or roses, and sometimes containing a Bible verse.

Miss Emy fanned herself as she drove. She required a fan at all times during the spring, summer, and fall. If the kitchen warmed too much during Thanksgiving and Christmas preparations, she took down one of the fans she kept hanging on the wall. If push came to shove, Miss Emy would also use a piece of cardboard from a 12-pack of Shasta as a fan and wave it back and forth in front of her face as we trolled the stalls at the Farmer's Market.

She told all of her friends to visit our booth and buy some of the produce and herbs, but mainly people bought items that she sewed—dresses, baby clothes, curtains, and quilts. I helped her with the quilting and tried to learn how to smock, but I wasn't that good at it. I always got too frustrated. When he was on a binge, I took over my Dad's part and made the preserves and collected the herbs. He was the forager and knew all the places on the property, outside of the medicine wheel, like where to find ginseng, yellow root, pokeweed, stinging nettle, cattail pollen, and a lot of wild herbs. He also kept up the medicine wheel and planted new lavender, ginger, rosemary, thyme, parsley, and many culinary and beauty product herbs. He created instructions for tinctures and compresses, tea recipes, and even poured candles into leaves of lemon balm. He shelled and bagged black walnuts, collected poppy seeds and mistletoe bundles. He didn't care what people expected and made no plans. Melinda said of him, "Whatever was in season, Daniel learned to work with nature, but he was never satisfied. He was eating away at himself, looking for heroin from dealers after our uncle died and no longer provided it to him. I just know that Daniel got it from our Daddy's brother."

Miss Emy sold most of what she took to the market every week and collected orders for sewing and for herb collections. If Dad couldn't collect, I filled in, and Miss Emy made certain to give me a percentage of his profit. "He's still the business owner," she'd say, "so he gets most of the money from the sale, but since you have done so much this time, you take 15%." Of course, I did more and more and grew older and wanted to keep more profit for myself, but Miss Emy knew that Dad would be around soon, raging for more money, if we didn't send him off with enough to suit him for a while. To me, he just blew through it faster and faster.

I learned about the plants and herbs, at first to follow my Dad around, and later, to help earn a profit, but never conceived of the potential healing or perceived the harm that they could cause until I was much older, and then, we had let it go, only giving some paper bags of rosemary, sage, or lavender to people while the plants were in season. Someone would come begging for ginseng or try to sneak on the property to forage for it in late August themselves. Miss Emy wasn't gifted with the desire to understand plant mysteries—the chemistry of the dark and twisted soil and roots, stones and sediments. She helped my Dad in his business, and from that learned more than ever before, opening herself enough to be healed of the fear she had cultivated because of Zona. And yet, she only dabbled and tasted swiftly, fluttering to dip in and partake of only the sweetest and safest of herbal remedies and recipes.

Miss Emy kept her change in a big, red glass jar with a metal lid. She kept the jar in the bottom of her chiffarobe and concealed by the hems of dresses and nightgowns that I had never seen Miss Emy wear. She was always in plain pants and a shirt. Solid color fabrics. She tried to maintain the farm and the family for such a long time. She found the time to take an animal to slaughter and sell the meat after keeping a few cuts. Some animals were used just to stock our deep freezer.

My Dad cared more about shooting up than doing the upkeep on the farm. Miss Emy said, "It's such a shame and a waste, but he's my son and I won't disown him."

My aunts always wanted her to show him tough love, to stop giving him money and supporting his lifestyle. They showed up together to confront their mother. Miss Emy was no longer in possession of some of her jewelry. The television was gone. The fancy china vanished. He wasn't keeping up with the crops anymore. When they stopped farming the tobacco fields, the fields gave way to a white wave of Queen Ann's lace, which turned brown and was overtaken by the purple ironweed. Wildness crept in from all corners.

"I'm not supporting his lifestyle," she said sternly over the kitchen table. "He knows I don't agree with it." My aunts sat around the table. Miss Emy stood and pointed me toward the stove, "You ready to start your cooking lesson today?" she asked me. She was teaching me some cooking basics, which distracted both of us and gave me a feeling of accomplishment. I skipped over to the stove. "Are we making the lasagna?" I asked.

"But Mama, don't you see that you're enabling his addiction?" Carolyn asked. She had given up cleaning products and makeup as part-time positions since her children were in school and she had taken a full-time position as a secretary at a rehabilitation center.

"I don't understand what you mean," Miss Emy said to Carolyn.

"If you give him money all the time, he thinks that he can always come back to you and get money and go buy more drugs. If you'd stop giving him money, and tell him that he wasn't going to get a damn penny until finishing a rehabilitation program, then he would learn that he doesn't have a choice. He has to stay off drugs."

I tried to interrupt Carolyn a few times, saying, "Miss Emy! Lasagna? Miss Emy?"

Miss Emy sat quietly with her hands around her coffee mug. She stared down at the wooden tabletop and looked up at me, "What do you think?" she asked. "You think it'd work?"

"You said we were making lasagna, Miss Emy!" I said, thinking that's what she meant.

"Ok, lasagna will be alright. Get the noodles out of the cabinet and use the big pot." As I turned on the faucet to put water in the pot for the noodles to boil, Miss Emy asked me again, "Do you think your Daddy needs to go somewhere to get help for his drug habit?"

My face burned hot. I thought that I might cry. I was only ten and all of my strategies had to do with escape, hiding, and survival. I shrugged as the water rose in the pot.

"Miss Emy," Melinda said as if she were correcting a child. "How's she supposed to know what to do? She's just ten years old. She doesn't know how to save him."

"That's probably enough water," Carolyn said to me, and I turned the faucet off. My back felt pinched when I tried to carry the big pot to the stove, and Miss Emy hurried from her seat to help me place it on top. She set the dial on High and instructed me to add salt to the pot, while saying to her daughters, "Well, I think she's just as smart as anybody else I know, and she's lived with him and learned how to deal with him better than anybody. I just thought…" she shook her head and waved her hand toward my aunts. "You all are frustrating me," she said abruptly, faced the coffee maker and added more to her cup. "I don't know what to do. He's gonna end up killing me with this. I kept thinking he'd outgrow it. It was just a bad habit. But, he's hooked on it, isn't he?" She turned to look at her daughters seated at the table. She picked up a fan and waved it in front of her face. The wind caused her collar to billow slightly.

"Yes, Mama, he is," Carolyn said. "I can tell you for certain. I've talked to too many people. Our pastor and people at our church who know about these things. They say that heroin is the worst thing you can do. The most addictive drug. And that shooting up with needles is the most addictive way to use drugs. He's not just going to get better on his own. He needs help, Mama. And you're really the only person who can convince him to get some help."

"Miss Emy, what can I do now?" I asked staring into the salted water.

"Put the top on it," she said to me. She looked at my aunts. "I don't know if I've got the strength for this," she said with a violent exhale that contained tears. She dropped the fan onto the counter.

I waited for a moment. "Miss Emy," I said timidly, "Now, what should I do for the lasagna?"

"Go get an onion, a green pepper, some tomatoes, three or four, and the hamburger meat," Carolyn said to me.

From the pantry, I listened to them. I also found garlic cloves with the onions and took a few of those because I had watched Miss Emy put them in spaghetti.

Melinda said, "You can do this. We can help you." Miss Emy was shaking her head and wiping tears away quickly. "Listen to me," Melinda continued. "You have to do this…for him. He's your baby boy, isn't he? You care about your child, don't you?"

"Well, yeah, you know that I do."

"Then, you can do this. You can convince him to go to a rehab program and get some help. There are people who can help him," Carolyn said. I returned with the vegetables.

Miss Emy waved her hands frantically, and expelled "Shhhh!" violently toward us while cutting her eyes toward the door. The fan began fluttering violently in front of her face.

Melinda stood to look through the window. "He's out there. I wonder if he heard you," she whispered. "He's just standing there, very still. You think he was listening?" She stood in a half squat to peek through the window again and sat down quickly with a scared giggle.

Miss Emy had been talking over her the whole time in a louder than normal voice, "I believe I need to make another pot of coffee. Are you staying for supper or heading back soon?" she asked Carolyn, but didn't give her time to answer. She just kept on talking in a continuous stream, "There's plenty of lasagna, and I knew Daniel would love it, especially with Robin learning to cook, she has to show off her new recipe."

He opened the door. "Well, there he is now," Miss Emy said.

"Yeah, what are you all talking about me for?" he asked suspiciously.

"I was telling them how much you like lasagna and we're having it for dinner tonight." She flapped the fan in slower strokes. "Robin is making it." I smiled and looked over my shoulder at my Dad. He crossed the room and kissed me on the top of my head.

"You got that right," he said. "I do like lasagna, but I can't stay tonight. I'll have some leftovers tomorrow." He patted the top of my head. "They say Italian food is better the next day. Cold pizza, day-old spaghetti. I bet lasagna is the same." He laughed. "Sorry I can't stay for the party tonight." He surveyed his sisters. "What are you all doing here anyway? Where's the kids?" He looked at Carolyn.

"Where you going?" Miss Emy asked him, but he didn't answer.

"Can I cut the onion, Miss Emy?" I asked, retrieving the cutting board and knife.

"They're at school," Carolyn said. "It's been a while since I've been to visit, and it just worked out for all of us today."

"Alright," he said. "I'm taking these biscuits with me and going back over to my house to get cleaned up. I won't see you 'til tomorrow sometime. Okay?" He reached onto the top of the stove and grabbed the four biscuits still sitting there from the morning. He kissed the top of my head again and said, "Be careful with that knife if you plan on cutting those vegetables."

"Let me have the knife, Robin," Miss Emy said to me, taking the cutting board and vegetables, too. She placed it all in front of Melinda, who immediately sliced straight through the onion.

I didn't stay at Dad's house anymore because I preferred to eat breakfast and every other meal at Miss Emy's, rather than cook it by myself. At that point, there wasn't any food there anyway, maybe something scarce, but probably not since he was taking the biscuits. Miss Emy tried for months to bring us food until it was just too much trouble. Things would ruin because I couldn't really cook more than an egg sandwich and a pack of bacon, and Dad was too messed up or gone most of the time. He was hung over a lot and just demanded coffee while holding his head in his hands. Miss Emy said that I might as well stay with her, and the food wouldn't ruin, and then nobody worried about whether or not I was hungry or by myself. He said that he had the same idea.

Dad said goodbye and opened the door to leave. Miss Emy said, "Don't forget that Robin is competing in the spelling bee tomorrow."

"I won't forget," he smiled toward me. "Sorry I gotta run," he said to his sisters, "but I'll see you all next time around." He could be the master of quick exchanges. That usually went better for him than having to sit down and talk to them, having to explain and speculate about politics, gossip, and religion, or having to explain his personal philosophy, which didn't always match theirs and which each of them labeled as "crazy" at some point. I have grown to think that we're all twisted up inside and can't articulate the imaginings and knowing of our perceptions and thoughts. We're lingering on an edge, looking down into a hollow that we swear is decorated with stars.

The first time I learned to stir a pot, my Daddy was making poke sallet. The boiled greens. He fried a whole chicken and even made himself a gizzard snack, drop biscuits, gravy and boiled potatoes. "The works" as he called it and laughed with his surprisingly deep pitch that had a slight pick-up on the end, as if he might get carried away in the laughter, but something in his eyes never quite let him. He told me, most importantly, you needed jowl to season the greens, boiling in there until finely torn to bits. He was a decent country cook, if he made a meal…but that wasn't often.

After he left, I asked, "What can I do now, Miss Emy?"

She didn't answer. She stared out the window in the direction where my Dad had left.

"He seems alright to me," Miss Emy said to them, fanning herself proudly after he left.

"You know it's only temporary," Melinda said. "I wish it wasn't, but it is."

"Miss Emy?" I pestered her. I'm not sure how many times I said it. "What can I do now?"

"We don't know that," Miss Emy said to Melinda.

"Miss Emy? The lasagna?" I nagged and whined.

"Take the lid off and stir the noodles," she said. They were finally boiling. I stood on a chair and used a pot holder as Miss Emy had taught me and lifted the lid off the pot of boiling water. I used a wooden spoon to stir the noodles.

"Don't fret," Carolyn said to me, "You've got your whole life to learn how to cook for a family. Besides, you don't even have one to cook for right now anyway." She only meant that I wasn't married. I wasn't a Mom with hungry kids, but Carolyn hit a wound and it stung so badly that I lost my train of thought, and when I dropped the spoon into the boiling water, my hand automatically reached in after it. I screamed. Miss Emy shrieked, while Melinda jumped up and down, panting,

They seemed to cry in unison, "Oh my God, Oh my God, Oh my God..." over and over.

Carolyn flung the cold water on full blast from the tap and shoved my hand underneath it. I tried to breathe in and felt some relief from the cold water. After that, I was led by the shoulders hurriedly and the car took us, crying and shaking, knees bouncing, wincing.

I tried to maintain my composure in the hospital. Didn't want to be like Dad in that way, suffering uncontrollable pain, and trying to peel the body away, just crawl right out of the skin to escape pain, or satisfy it by crawling more deeply into it. I just thought about everything else, disconnecting some line. Blank. Blank. Blank. Fields. Blank. Miss Emy's hem is never exactly even on anything she sews. Cluck. Cluck. Geese. Blank. Blank. I could see that needle stitching up and down. Then I could hear that sewing machine. The foot. Trying not to think about my hand in a fast stream where the hand screams in whelps, leaping and bounding out of its place, stricken with a panic while the lash overpowers. I kept thinking about when we cooked that meal, my Dad and I.

I tried not to think about Miss Emy and my aunts. Miss Emy flapping that fan in the car, trying to fan my hand, saying, "It'll be okay. It'll be okay," and asking, "What happened?" I just said, "I don't know," but that only made me cry, and I was trying not to cry out and scream at the end of the tears—little shrieks reached my lips in a relentless inability to keep my bubbling, peeling flesh from speaking in the only way it could. "See, you just see," Carolyn said to Miss Emy, "she should've been playing with a friend somewhere, not dealing with all these grownup responsibilities." Melinda agreed and hugged me in the backseat. "It all his fault!" she screamed suddenly at Miss Emy.

I wanted to block them out and tried not to think at all. And then, I realized that I had been treated quickly at the hospital and was starting to feel the weight of drugs moving through my body. My eyelids began slumping as I stared at Miss Emy on the ride back home. "It's okay. Nobody's fault," I tried to squeeze out of my lips with a smile.

Miss Emy was there, sitting in the chair beside my bed, when I woke up. "You feel alright?"

"I'm okay," I said.

"You were tough and barely even cried."

"I don't remember," I said.

My aunts picked up a new television set while I was being treated at the hospital, and Miss Emy finished the lasagna with the two of them. They spent the night, and I had almost forgotten about the need for an intervention. After my accident, they rallied around me so that I wanted it to remain that cozy—was actually believing they had traveled to visit me in the first place.

Even though I didn't win and my Dad didn't show up, I looked out from the stage of the spelling bee and at my aunts. Both sat in the audience with Miss Emy. I didn't want anything to change, and then he passed through the door and startled us, as if he were a shadow that moved. Said he was there to check on me, heard the news from someone in town who worked at the hospital. First, my aunts were gone as quickly as they arrived. And then, he disappeared, with my pain medication. I didn't care since I forgot to take it anyway.

Miss Emy didn't forget and asked me about it. I told her that it was gone when she said that she wanted to count the pills. I explained quickly so as not to cry, "I didn't take it. I don't take it." Though I did cry.

"I know it's not you, Robin," Miss Emy said. Of course, she knew the real culprit and reassured me about her suspicion in the first place. Part of me tried to protect my Dad when given the chance.

I guess that's part of the reason why I got the reputation around town—popular for being strong. I didn't really cry when I put my hand in the boiling water. My aunt Melinda wailed more than I did. She was sentimental and worried more than anyone else in the family.

"She worries enough for generations to come," Miss Emy said. She always had something to say about Melinda, and then, I suppose, those people (like Melinda) with high-reaching aspirations give us all a reason to try to describe them.

I picked at my hand, and it wouldn't heal. Picking. Picking. Scratching and shedding. I wanted to play the guitar for a distraction, but I couldn't.

Time passed and Miss Emy fanned herself, cooked for people, paced around the yard, chased after my Dad to care for something on the farm, and finally, she started selling the livestock. Once the animals were gone, she sold everything that went with them. She kept the old pickup truck, the tractor, and bush hog.

They did try, several times in the next year, to intervene and coax him into a rehab center. Aunt Carolyn talked to my Dad by herself. They walked down the road three times, and spent all afternoon talking about the program at the place where she worked, but he didn't go, even though he told her that he'd come up there and talk to someone in person. She assured him that everything is private, and she wouldn't have any knowledge of his files, and that he could leave anytime—they couldn't keep him there. He had to sign himself in and he could sign out whenever he wanted to. It was a voluntary program. She told me and Miss Emy about it before she talked to him. I was worried that he'd get mad at her and scream and yell, but he didn't. They seemed to have a good talk and after all that time they spent walking, I maintained hope that he would get help. Aunt Carolyn told us that he had confided in her. Betrayal and withdrawal from family were getting to him, as well as his lack of money and watching many of his prosperous friends pass him by in their business and family endeavors.

About two months later, he started the program, but he didn't stay. After a month, he called Miss Emy to come pick him up. We'd already been to a family visitation the day before, and Miss Emy said that our visitation was probably the problem. We shouldn't have gone and made him think about Granville.

He went right out and bought drugs. Begged Miss Emy for money all the time. We had to hide the money or he'd just take it. His face was chiseled out, and sometimes hollowed with dark embedded places. He didn't eat very much when we saw him, and at that point, he was maintaining his ability to be pleasant, but that didn't last many more years. Sometimes, he erupted in a rage, and I'd hide while Miss Emy tried to reason with him until she basically paid him to leave, to go away and find some drugs.

I walked into his room a few times when he was cooking his drugs on the spoon. He never noticed me in the doorway. He was so intensely focused, and I guess you'd have to be if you didn't want to mess up and lose some of what you were making, some of what he sacrificed everything to get and use. It seemed as if his invisible life force kept him alive, as if I could actually catch a glimpse of the blood move through his veins and surge into his heart. He felt that way, and maybe all addicts do, but I could see a look of want that I'd never seen on his face for anything else while he was preparing. Without it, I imagined him shriveling up like a plant without nutrients. His insides would sink into darkness. I shuddered under the weight of that image, even if his muscles were tan and veined and controlled at that point. Some knowing slithered and pulsed. When I stood in the doorway and stared at him, I was mesmerized, really. He looked like a magician. It wasn't very bright in his room, but he was lit up, as if he were electric in anticipation, but maybe I've made it more luminous than it was. He sat on the edge of the bed, the quilt frayed in places. An old, vintage white lamp with a huge, round shade stood on the table that looked more like a child's nightstand beside his bed. Ashtrays were on the little nightstand, on the floor, on the bed, and in front of the closet. Miss Emy went in there once a week and collected them. It smelled like ash, even when the window was open. He did have blue curtains, and they were nice, surprisingly. Miss Emy told me that she bought them for him one year for Christmas.

He was brown with perfect chestnut hair that glinted from the sun's touch. His big eyes were kind and full when he was the man I was proud to call my Dad. Standing in his doorway, I could never see his eyes at all. He was focused and his veins swelled, and I felt like I could see the motion in them. Maybe it's just because he tried to keep his arms covered with long-sleeve shirts when he was using so much. And, he eventually blew out the veins in them anyway, couldn't catch them to fill them after a while. I wanted to hold his hand, but he was self-conscious, even when he was clean.

****

It didn't take a long time for the house to burn down. We could see some smoke curling in the distance, but just thought it must've been a campfire somewhere in the hollow where there were a few hunting cabins. The smoke kept coming, and it rolled with a dark knowing that we recognized after fifteen minutes. We started down the path slowly, trying to reassure each other that the smoke was a campfire, but with each step, our voices reflected our fear. We got to the driveway, gravelly and bumpy, and the fire rolled across the landscape, between the trees. Miss Emy said, "I don't know if that's a campfire or not. I don't have a good feeling about that smoke." We got closer to my Dad's house, and the smoke was coming up fast toward Miss Emy's.

"We've got to go back and call 9-1-1!" She shouted because she'd already turned around and was running back in the direction of her house. She already knew that Dad's house was on fire. "It'll take ten minutes for the fire truck and the police to get over there," Miss Emy said. "We better go back and make sure your Dad is alright."

"Do you think his house is on fire?" I shouted to her. "Is that why you're calling 9-1-1?"

"It's a lot of smoke that doesn't smell like a campfire and I could hear glass breaking. I don't know." Miss Emy ran.

It suddenly occurred to me that my Dad could be inside of the house. I turned and ran down the hill path and then down the road toward the house.

I could hear crackling and popping, like trees falling. I wondered if he caught the woods on fire somehow. I was hopeful, not wanting to face the house until I did see its frame glowing, and dark smoke pouring back into itself until it overflowed and rolled out onto the landscape.

"Dad!" I shouted. "Dad!" I ran around the yard, to the other side of the house. "Dad!" I yelled into the fire. I screamed. "Where are you?" I cried.

The flames flicked out of the once hollow spaces of the house. Miss Emy suddenly grabbed my shoulder and pulled me backward, away from the burning house. She hugged me. "I'm so sorry. I pray to God he wasn't in there. I love you, Robin. I'm so sorry." I cried and we fell back into the grass, watching the house burn. After a few minutes, we heard the sirens, and Miss Emy stood, started waving her hands over her head as if they didn't know where to go.

My Dad wasn't there, after all, and we didn't know where he was for three hours. Miss Emy tried to find him, but everyone said they hadn't seen him. The fire inspector eventually determined that faulty electrical wiring had caused it. In my mind, I could see my Daddy messing up the wires, making a spark, and getting out of there as quickly as possible. He seemed too nonchalant about the whole incident.

Aunt Melinda came to pick me up so that I could spend a week with her in Nashville. She said, "You don't think he would do it on purpose to get the insurance money, do you, Miss Emy? It doesn't matter because either way, he'll get the money."

"You beat all I've ever seen. His house just burned down and he's lost everything, and all you can think is that your own brother is a criminal. All your life, you've been accusing him of something. Accused him of beating up on Robin or hurting her when she was little, and he never laid a hand on that child. Accused him of stealing from me that time somebody broke in and took the television and china and stuff."

"I think if it was a bunch of thieves, they would've taken other valuables, not just pick and choose some things he thought he could get away with," Aunt Melinda said. "He only limited himself because he felt guilty for doing it. I don't trust him."

"Well, I do, and I don't want to hear any more about it!" Miss Emy said. "The fire chief said what caused the fire. If they were suspicious of him, they would've wanted to question him, and they aren't, so that's enough."

"I'm just looking out for Robin's best interest," Melinda said. "It's not good that he doesn't work or contribute anything. That's a terrible example to her." She pointed to me, and I felt so sick.

"This isn't the best for her either," Miss Emy said. "You sitting around here pointing the finger at her Daddy."

"She's old enough to know he's not right," Melinda said. "She knows he's on drugs."

"Yeah, but that's still her Daddy," Miss Emy said. "I don't know if she needs to stay with you or not." I wished that Aunt Melinda would stop talking so that we could leave. I wanted to visit her in Nashville instead of moping around the farm, and it still smelled like smoke to me, especially if I got close to the side where Dad's house was.

"Do we make you feel bad when we talk about your Dad?" Aunt Melinda asked me.

I just shrugged my shoulders. "You can tell me," she said.

"Sometimes," I said, "but it's not because of you. It's because of him." I didn't want to cry, but the tears just came up fast and my shoulders were shaking before I had a chance to hide everything. Aunt Melinda wrapped her arms around me and then I cried for a long time. She said, "Let's just stop talking about it then. You and I are going to have such a good time. I've got some fun stuff planned for us. You like roller coasters?"

I shrugged.

"You don't like them or you don't know if you do or not?"

"I've never been on one," I said, and began to cry again. I couldn't seem to turn off the emotions once they began.

"Really?" she looked surprised. "You're fourteen," she said, as if I didn't know my own age. "Time to change that," she said. "As long as you want to ride one with me. It's fun." She smiled and patted my leg, squeezed my shoulder. "Let's grab your stuff and get going."

The first stop we made was a used clothing boutique in Nashville, where Aunt Melinda scooted the hangers rapidly and held clothes up to my body. She pressed a sequined gown against my breasts and angled the waistline against my stomach. It matched my skin tone, so she told me to try it on.

"What's it for?" I asked.

"You," she said.

"Where would I wear something like this?"

"We'll find an event," she said. "Now, try on the other clothes too, and hurry up, because we have an appointment with my hairdresser."

I giggled and then clapped a hand over my mouth quickly.

She looked at me with pity, and said, "Oh, Robin, baby girl, it's okay to be happy. Don't ever stop yourself from laughing, unless it's at an old person and you don't want to hurt their feelings." She hugged me when I began to cry again. "No more crying," she said with a smile. "This is a fun time. We're saying goodbye to the blues and hello to happiness. You know why? Because I got dumped by my boyfriend for another woman two days ago…"

"Oh, I'm sorry, Aunt Melinda," I interrupted.

But she just continued, "…and I refuse to feel sorry for myself. I will find someone better than him, dirt bag!" She laughed. "Try on clothes, try on clothes," she said holding up a short, navy blue dress. "This is a classic. Versace," she said. "You'll have it forever, if you take care of it."

I didn't know anything about brands or fashion beyond the popular—Guess brand jeans and how we were supposed to wear them.

Aunt Melinda decided we would overcome tragedy, and that's why she wanted me to stay with her instead of going to be with my cousins at Aunt Carolyn's. "They'll just want to talk about it over and over, until you get sick of it. And, they're constantly driving to ball fields and practices with those kids, and you'd just be along for the ride. Staying with me, you're the priority."

That week, we went to Opryland for three days. I think I screamed from pure joy that we were going for thirty solid seconds when she told me the next morning at dawn. She was going to beat the crowd, and park at the front of the parking lot, or we would "have to walk a mile just to get to the trolley station," Aunt Melinda explained. "We get first dibs on the rides, too."

We were headed straight for the biggest and best, she explained. "The legendary Wabash Cannonball," she said with a huge smile. "You'll go upside down on it." She revealed and giggled.

"How can we go upside down?" I asked. "Very funny. You're joking with me."

"Not at all," she said. "But don't you worry, they'll have us all strapped in and everything. You won't fall out." She laughed and patted my back, urging me forward on our journey to the legendary rollercoaster.

"Oh, let's just stop right now, and ride the log ride," she said. "I can't help myself, but I love this one—the Flume Zoom. You will, too. It's so fun and not scary at all." She put her hands on my shoulder blades and guided me into the empty lanes for the water log ride. We climbed up, high above the park in our Lincoln log on the waterway. Music started below us and singers harmonized their voices. Aunt Melinda explained that Opryland prided itself on being the musical launching pad for many young musicians starting out in country music. And then we dipped suddenly, and I yelled and laughed along with Aunt Melinda, and we bounced and bobbled as the water sprinkled and sprayed us until our log leveled out on the track and floated into the stall. The line was short with only one group in front of us after our log was filled, so Aunt Melinda suggested that we ride it again. I nodded enthusiastically.

I wanted to stop at other rides on the way to her Wabash Cannonball, but she wouldn't allow it. "We have just enough time," she said. "It doesn't go over and over like the logs. It's only once an hour, and during the busy times, twice an hour."

"Oh," I said, my shoulders slumping.

"But don't worry," she said. "We'll make it, and we can ride it as many times as you want, but I'll bet that in the end, you'll want to go on the log ride more."

"Hey! I'm not a scaredy cat!" I said.

"You'll see," she said.

The iron bar clicked into place, and I listened to the other riders behind us, telling tales about the cannonball— the loopedy loops, and what if the bar broke or it just came right off the track. What makes it stay on the track? Nobody knows. Gears. Something like big rubber bands. Springs and magnets. Remember to take off your sunglasses and make sure that nothing can fall out of pockets or off your body or clothes. "It would fall on someone's head?" I whisper to Aunt Melinda. "That's really scary." My knees bounced on the metal, and I bit my fingernails. I spit the nails out.

"Just relax. It'll be fun. Here we go!" Aunt Melinda squeezed my knee. The rollercoaster cars clicked forward and around the corner, into the outside light, away from the sheltered structure where the cars slept and more people waited. They watched us with longing, apprehension, and their own desire for adrenaline. We turned another corner and began to click up, up, up, up. I looked over the edge and trembled. "It's so far down there," I said. Aunt Melinda looked over her side. "I always forget how far it is," she laughed. "This is so fun! Oh, here we go! Here we go!" she said almost breathlessly as we neared the edge of a precipice. I couldn't see where it went, and I saw hair fly up and arms rise in instinctive reach for anything in the air to grab, and we were free-falling, screaming, fast, and we straightened out with speed for a moment, until we spun and floated above the chair swings flying out in an arc, and we were back upright for a speeding instant of clouds and blue sky and each other's smiling faces, and upside down again and people pointed from the sidewalk below. We spun around in a whirl and screeched forward. Rocked. Slower. Bumped. I smoothed my hair and clothes with wild laughs. "I'm going to raise my hands over my head next time we're upside down," I told Aunt Melinda. She agreed, and we did it. She was like a kid.

We flared out our legs together on the big swings and spun around and around. She hopped into the passenger seat of the old timey cars at Tin Lizzie and let me drive, following the metal track around the lawns, gliding between some trees and shrubs, away from the crowds and lines for a moment, as if we were transported into the countryside—the cardinals even flitted among the branches to make us believe it for a moment. The train whistled, and I steered us along the track and back into the station.

We stood in a long line and the clouds thickened overhead, drawing out the mosquitoes near the tropical plants they'd added along the path where the line grows.

The Screamin' Delta Demon sound effects annoyed us, and we were hungry, uncomfortable, and itchy by the time we'd slogged through the demon's cavern and exited the ride.

Aunt Melinda's big bag, which was a purse with a drawstring on the top, was loaded with everything we would possibly need, except food, and we were going to buy food. "Definitely, buying food," she said, fishing through her purse for her wallet. "If you try and bring your food, someone has to sit with it, or you leave it in the car and go back for it. Pack a cooler. Rent a locker. All of them are a hassle. We are only doing this for three days, so we're buying our lunch at a restaurant, and they have a lot of them." We chose the one by the Tin Lizzies that was like a tea house. "Perfect. Delightful. This hits the spot, and we don't have any baggage to deal with," Aunt Melinda said at the table of the restaurant. At first I wanted to be part of the other families picnicking around on park benches until I watched them eyeing for free tables and scrambling when one became vacant for a second, and I was happy that she and I could sit at a table all to ourselves and not feel like we had to let it go or race another family. We could stay there, while she drank four cups of tea, and I slurped on two and a half sodas, and we knew that we were wanted, and I could see that the girl with half her family slumped on the park bench and half of them on the sidewalk wanted to be at a table with my aunt with a perfect view of the field filled with old timey cars and with the music sounding just right. I smiled at the girl, and just then, her sandwich that she placed on a napkin on the sidewalk by her leg was almost smashed by a few groups crowding by. I watched the commotion of legs and feet, and her hands quickly snatched the sandwich. She immediately bit into it, as she eyed the trespassers.

Aunt Melinda patted my leg and pointed to the banana split on the table in front of us. My eyes widened, and I let go of the straw in my mouth and placed the soda on the table.

We played at the amusement park for two more days, which were full of humidity by the bandstands, stages, and lines, soaking wet clothes from the Grizzly River Rampage, sticky fingers and lips from funnel cakes and New York seltzers. I was floating on the Cumberland in a colorful, sweet nostalgia—I'd just come to live with my Aunt Melinda, strolling the avenues of Nashville, buying one of those season passes to Opryland so that we could ride the Wabash every weekend, sitting backstage at the Opry while she interviewed a young country music artist for *Music City Mornings*, and going to a new school where I could be Melinda Ballard's niece, and I secretly hoped they would believe I was her daughter. I watched the singers and guitar players on the backstage of the Opry. Maybe they thought I was her daughter. They talked to me, and I thought my heart would leap out onto the stage, and then, they'd say, "I just love your aunt. She's a fun lady. I bet you like staying with her, don't you?"

I kept imagining myself in that new life with every click and turn of a rollercoaster or turnstile. Except for the bumper cars—I detested those and their racket. I was blindsided in an instant and given whiplash from an eight-year-old boy with a demonic laugh. Then, a whole group of teenage boys blocked us in for the final two minutes of the bumper car time, and two minutes of bumper bruising by acne-faced, cackling boys feels way too long. That was the second day and the only time I would have described as *bad*.

The third day was bliss-filled—I spilled some purple slushy on my white shorts, but my shoulders shrugged as we wound up the dark hallway, up, up, up. They sold concessions—ice cream, pretzels, kettle chips, and Crunch 'n' Munch, along one side of the hallway that continued higher until reaching a single-file platform in a dark, enclosed tower room. I sensed some abyss, but it was called Chaos, and we sat in the rollercoaster and awaited the show. The rollercoaster jerked around in frenetic movements while black-and-white ghostly photographic images flickered on screens. A random fire. A scream. A yelp. Minimal surrealism swirling and jerking us around. Aunt Melinda said, "Could be interesting if it wasn't so boring. Good concept, though. Maybe they'll perfect it." After a few minutes of trying to decide what to ride next, she looked toward the entrance to the building and said, "Let's ride it again."

Inside the Chaos building, Aunt Melinda ate ice cream and shivered. I stared at another family in line—the mom leaned against the wall underneath one of the lights. Her blonde hair lit up like a halo. The two sisters finished their ice cream dots and huddled close to their mom's legs. The light illumined the goose bumps on their arms and legs. I turned around and faced another family.

"Thank you for bringing me to do this, Aunt Melinda," I said suddenly.

She put her arms around me and leaned against an empty space along the wall. "I've had so much fun with you," she said.

She was great at that—giving me opportunities to have fun. I would have missed out on movies and roller coasters, fashion and hairstyles, the TV and radio world, without Aunt Melinda. When given the choice (and I was always quizzed by Miss Emy, as well as Aunt Carolyn), I asked to be with Melinda. She and I danced in the car and sang all the popular music as loudly as possible, even rapping with LL Cool J underneath her open sunroof. She let me stick my head out the top when we drove slowly downtown, and some people on the sidewalk waved, so I felt like I was in a parade, imagining wearing that fancy dress, so big it filled the inside of the car, and my gloved hand waving and waving to the pedestrians, the children pointing and smiling.

We drove down West End Avenue, and she'd point toward Interstate 40, where the buildings downtown rose up to form a city skyline, nothing like the pictures of New York I'd seen, but it sure beat the courthouse in Granville. As we circled I-40 in Nashville, there was one skyscraper building bigger than the others with messages written using the window lights. Aunt Melinda said, "That's the Tennessee Tower." I was mesmerized. My face pressed to the passenger side glass of the car. The workers left the office lights on inside the Tennessee Tower to form a message that travelers could read as they passed through

the city. The first message I read was "You are the Light."
Over the years, I read the words "Travel Safe", "God is
Love", and even "Friday!" once. The Christmas message
was always "Peace." Aunt Melinda drove the city loop two
or three times to let me stare at the lights. She gave me
such freedom to play and enjoy little moments.

As hip as Aunt Melinda tried to be, though, her one
cheesy love was Elvis. She was one of those fans,
dedicating a whole room in her house to him. Or maybe,
she felt the need to hide her affair with Elvis in one room.
Her "dancing room," as she called it. She played Elvis
records. Of course, she owned a great stash of other jazz
and blues records, but she was dedicated to Elvis. His
photographs hung on the walls. The room was quite
modern, elegant, and spacious. She'd visited Graceland a
few times and knew some facts by heart. Aunt Melinda's
personal favorites were his recording of "Blue Moon of
Kentucky", which she quickly pointed out "was written by
Bill Monroe, aka the God of bluegrass and recorded by
Elvis in 1954. And, the song recorded the same year,
'That's All Right' is my other favorite." She put on the
record, "That's all right now, Mama, any way you do!"
And we sang our hearts out in the 1968 way, wanting to
leave town in black leather jackets just because it seemed
like the action that fit the picture, but we didn't. Aunt
Melinda's ideas were contagious, and I fell in lust with
young Elvis at a time when my peers thought Kurt Cobain
was the divine guitar guy.

Three years later, the dancing room became Great
Aunt Cora's place. After she had her knees replaced, she

auctioned her farm and most of the contents, believing that to be her only choice, before Aunt Melinda had an opportunity to protest. For almost a decade, Aunt Cora's caregiver was one of her brother's daughters who helped Aunt Cora tend the farm, but as the years passed, she cared for Aunt Cora less and slowly fell victim to her own greed for Aunt Cora's money until she succeeded in stealing thousands. When my Aunt Melinda discovered that Aunt Cora was in a nursing home, Aunt Melinda convinced her to leave the same day, and she hired a lawyer to go after the stolen money.

"I straighten out messes in life," Aunt Melinda said. "I've got a talent for knowing when to swoop in, and somehow it works out in the person's favor. I believe it always will when I have that hunch and act on it."

She can find the best treasures, and that means people, especially. She also respected handmade gifts and understood the small creations and the impact of the moments when they are given. On one of my visits as a young girl spending a weekend with her, she gave me a rare uplift into specialness, something I watched my peers and cousins receive from their parents—reassurance that they were special children, special people, even talented. These parents exuded a pride that I only encountered elusively.

Aunt Melinda and I sat on her porch stairs, watching people pass on the street, going back and forth to shopping centers (one on 46th Avenue), and the school and church. The brown brick stack from the old snuff building stood behind us. Someone whistled from the other side of the sunflowers as he passed on the sidewalk. My grandpa Paul planted the mammoth sunflowers in front of the fence, along the sidewalk, "to brighten up the street," so Aunt Melinda has maintained his tradition every year.

While we sat in the afternoon sun, looking out at the sunflowers and motion of the street, she placed a small box on my lap. I hesitated, but she said, "Open it, silly." Inside the box, the chain fell forward to a point from the top corners. The point held a dainty teardrop, a gleaming golden drip with a bright diamond in the center.

"I bought this for your Mom after she had you," Aunt Melinda said. Tears filled her eyes. "Sorry," she smiled and batted her eyelashes. "But then, well, you know. I'm so sorry." She took a deep breath and touched my shoulder. "I want to tell you why this is special," she said. "I never gave it to her, and this was before I had a lot of money, but I did save enough to go into the Service Merchandise store in Nashville and buy this for her." She laughed. "She just seemed so pitiful," Aunt Melinda stifled her own laughter quickly, once that word escaped from her mouth, and continued adding quickly, "and she needed to feel special." She touched my head. "You've just got to live life—for her. I thought that I should give it to you now, that you're older." She took the necklace out of the box and put it around my neck while I held my hair out of the way. She cried and hugged me while I sobbed. She cupped my face in her hands, and then held onto the necklace for a moment, "So proud of you, and I just know you're going to accomplish whatever you want in life."

She wiped the tears away from both of our faces. "What do you think you want to do?"

"Go to college," I said.

"What will you study?"

I shrugged.

"There's plenty of time to decide," she said.

"I just hope I can pay for it," I said.

"I didn't think you were old enough to think like that," she said.

I knew that the necklace would be beautiful with a dress I would wear for my high school prom where I could surprise everyone and become the Queen, and I would wear it again for my college graduation, and all my big moments. It let me think about the life I wanted but didn't have.

Aunt Melinda helped me to choose the first milestone, which was bigger than a prom and entailed a plan for me to win enough money to get started at a university. "We'll figure out the rest later," she said over the phone. "You can win this and that'll start the ball rolling." I was back at home with Miss Emy and in a winter slump after spending so many hopeful summers with Aunt Melinda, and never receiving a permanent invitation to live with her. I was afraid to ask, and she never offered. Somewhere inside I knew that if Aunt Melinda wanted me to live with her and thought it would be a good idea, she would have suggested it, but every summer I packed my clothes into the suitcase, along with all my new treasures from our adventures, and watched silently through the car windows on the winding route back to Granville. She always reminded me, "I'll be back in a couple of weeks and you can spend the weekends. We'll go to the Nutcracker at Christmas and do all of our holiday fun stuff." She smiled and hugged me, but that was the extent of our conversation concerning my visitation schedule with her.

****

Early the spring of my senior year in high school, at the urging of Aunt Melinda, I signed up as a contestant for the beauty pageant at the Poke Sallet Festival. I wanted to win the scholarship prize money, a guaranteed two thousand dollars plus fifty percent of the donations at the door on the night of the pageant. "Did you plan this?" I asked Aunt Melinda when she suggested I wear the sequined gown that she insisted I try on the previous year.

"I wish I had that kind of psychic ability." She laughed. "You do look beautiful, and it fits you perfectly," she said.

My aunt Carolyn, who had just given birth for the fifth time, brought her family for the festival, so Miss Emy's house was full of wild chases, a whiny baby's screaming, inquiries about food and more food, and complaints that "this place is boring." Miss Emy sent them outside to the swing, and one of my cousins would dig and scratch at the dirt with a stick, another would yell at the cows, and someone always picked Miss Emy's flowers or trampled them.

Aunt Carolyn knocked on the door. "Wow!" she exclaimed when she saw me in the dress. "That's beautiful. You look amazing." She wiped away a few tears that fell down her cheeks. "We're so proud of you." She hugged me.

Aunt Melinda opened the door, "You're already dressed to go. Oh my, Robin, you look so glamorous."

"Thank you," I smiled timidly. Even though Aunt Melinda coached me for a month of weekends about being confident and walking straight—"stop hunching over," she said, "keep your back long"—I was uneasy about what other people would think about my appearance. Like a bull in a china shop was how I felt...in unfamiliar shoes, clothes, and everything. I wasn't sure I could pull it off— being a pageant girl, and good enough to win.

"What are you doing for the talent portion?" Aunt Carolyn asked.

"Singing," I said.

"Oh," she said. "I didn't know you could sing. I mean, like that."

"She has a wonderful voice," Aunt Melinda said. "She's just shy about it. Are you playing the guitar, too, like we talked about?"

"Yep," I said. "I've been practicing."

"You play the guitar too?" Aunt Carolyn asked. "Where did you learn to play? Are you in the band?"

"I just taught myself to play by listening to music. I can't play a lot," I said.

Her expression was a combination of concern and pity, and she changed the subject quickly, "Did you fix your own hair or did Melinda do it for you?" Aunt Carolyn asked.

"I did it myself, and she put a few of the bobby pins where I couldn't reach." They sat on the bed in my room. I finished applying my lip liner and lipstick.

"It looks professional," Aunt Carolyn said. "You might want to enter another pageant after this one. You're so pretty." It was quiet, and I began to tremble in the anticipation. "Do you have any jewelry to wear?" Aunt Carolyn asked. "I have a pair of earrings that I thought you might like to wear."

"Thanks, but I'm wearing Aunt Melinda's diamond earrings, and the necklace she gave me. It matches the dress perfectly." I put on the earrings in front of the mirror.

"I'll help you put it on," Aunt Melinda said.

I opened the jewelry box and pulled the little drawer forward, but the necklace wasn't there. I looked across the dresser, scanning every inch of the top. I squatted to look under the dresser, but couldn't get in a good position since the dress was so tight. "I always leave it in the jewelry box," I said. "I haven't worn it. Not ever. I only tried it on once with the dress, when you were here last weekend, and I put it right back in the drawer," I said to Aunt Melinda.

"I remember," she said.

Aunt Carolyn looked under the dresser, but it wasn't there. She lifted the bed skirt and looked around the bed, but she didn't find it either. We scoured the room until someone ran downstairs to check with Miss Emy and everyone else in the house. I cried and mascara streaked my face with gray. The sisters looked at one another, and their eyes hardened. I knew what they were thinking, and I thought it was true when Miss Emy said, "I had a bad feeling when he came by here yesterday."

"He wanted to see my dress," I sobbed. "I took him upstairs to see it."

"Did you show him the necklace?" Aunt Melinda asked.

"No, but he has always known about it," I said. "He probably didn't even remember what it was—that Aunt Melinda bought it for Mama. He was just looking for something to take. He was twitching and jumpy, nervous, so I know he just took it." I was sobbing and shaking.

Aunt Carolyn placed a towel under my chin so that makeup and tears wouldn't stain my dress.

Aunt Melinda tried to be optimistic, "Let's go look in your room one more time?"

We walked upstairs and looked everywhere. Miss Emy was so sorry. They were all sorry, but it was time to leave for the festival.

Aunt Melinda took off her necklace and placed it in my hand. "If you like this one, you can have it with the earrings. They go together." The single diamond solitaire gleamed and seemed to pierce through to my chest, to my confidence, and I surged with pity, but I heard that word that Melinda had said about my mother ring in my ears, "pitiful," so I washed my face in cold water. The cold was resolve—hardening, and I imagined my emotion as frozen, my confidence as solid steel. I reapplied my makeup. I was more determined to take the stage, and prove that I was different from my Dad and my Mama—I was worth more than I experienced, and I would go to a university so that I could buy as many necklaces as I desired, and no one would describe me or my life as "pitiful."

I glowed in the golden gown. The other contestants fluffed and ruffled as flowers, roses and lilies, carnations and hollyhocks. I would not wilt among them. I would gild myself in glints and gleams, growing more radiant and illumined with my body and my mind as I glided across the stage. I did not bobble, but pressed each heel in like a light anchor and twirled in a steady motion of light, rocking each hip with its potential range like wind wafting the petals. My neck lengthened as a stem to the sun.

Time for the cutting, and we waited backstage while they decided who would make it on to the next level. Fretting and evaluating, the contestants, including me, went over each step and misstep, and discussed how we perceived the judges and their styles. Someone shouted into the hairspray-filled room, "It's time," and we crammed out of the doorway, lifting our dresses, trying not to step on the other hemlines, except for Leslie Madison, who purposely tried to trip us and step on our hemlines, tangle our hair in another girl's dress. She didn't make a secret about her wishes for us to fail, so she practically threatened us with a mischievous smile, "Are you wondering what I might do to sabotage you?" She giggled with a gleam in her eye. "I switched out their eye shadows with each other when they were in the bathroom, since they had the same brand but different colors," she whispered to me backstage, while pointing at two girls in front of us. She laughed at her own antics and even recruited another girl to step on the thread hanging from a preoccupied girl's dress and snickered as the red thread grew longer until she picked up her toe and the girl walked onto the stage. I was happy that Leslie had to walk in front of me, and I didn't need eyes in the back of my head.

We formed three rows on the stage and awaited the top 20, as more than half would be cut. I was near the center and remained tall under the lights that warmed me and cast sparkles and tiny rainbows on the stage floor around me. Little spotlights bounced off the other girls and encircled them in reflections of rainbows and bubbles of light. Some of the girls rocked on stage, while others smiled tensely. Leslie waved to her family and blew a few kisses into the audience. I wondered if I looked like a mannequin, since I felt like plaster and plastic and paint as I both anchored myself to the stage floor and refused to move and planned my exit after the top 20 were called. I don't know what the announcer was saying before that, but he started calling out the names of the finalists who would continue in the pageant. "This is in no particular order, folks. I'll just jump right out and get this second round narrowed down. Number one is Millie Anderson. Number two is Leslie Jenkins. Number three…" I didn't hear the next name because I was too busy laughing inside at Leslie Madison who had forgotten there was another Leslie and started to walk away from her place on the stage and had to turn around and go back. She shrugged playfully and tapped her foot, as if she was thinking, *Ha-ha, that was funny, now call my name already.*

I was still wondering if he would call her name when he said, "Number sixteen is Robin Ballard." I was startled, and I think the audience realized it and they reacted. I could hear some of their comments while we stood at the front of the stage, "Isn't that sweet?" "She sure didn't expect to get picked. You can see it on her face." "She's a pretty little thing, isn't she?"

I didn't even notice the final names that were called, but I was relieved to discover that Leslie Madison was ranting backstage about why she wasn't chosen and "should have definitely been in the top twenty!" she shouted to her two friends, scooped her belongings into her arms, and pushed her way through the other contestants at the doorway, bumping them and knocking a girl into the doorframe and causing someone else to fall down to the floor. "Sorry," she laughed and continued without looking back. In the hallway, we heard her voice echo in a laugh, "Well, no, I'm not. Ha-ha."

A sigh escaped from most of us, once the "fallen" had recovered. After Leslie Madison left the scene, the absence of her dominance and disturbances created an atmosphere of support and encouragement. Some of the girls who weren't chosen stuck around to help us in and out of our dresses and clothes. We watched over each other after that, not allowing anyone to step on hemlines or pull strings. We said, "You have lipstick on your teeth." "Your bra is showing under your arm right there." "Practice speaking louder so they can hear your answer." "You shout when you talk. You should try not to shout when you answer the judge's question." "I like the second dance better than the first." We helped each other to prepare for the talent portion. Most of us were singing or dancing, or both, for some.

Everyone knew that Leslie Jenkins's voice was beautiful and like an angel. We said, "Oh, she'll win for sure. There's no doubt about this part of the contest." I was relieved that I would be on stage before she sang, as I figured that would give me a chance to get a score from the judges that was independent of a comparison to Leslie. Everyone in Granville knew about her voice—she had a reputation as the singer, and sang the national anthem at all the ball games. She wasn't sweating or fretting like the rest of us. Each time I practiced the song, I fumbled the guitar chords and made an awful noise at least once. I didn't want it to squeak at all. Practicing backstage was messing me up—what with all the other girls who were tap dancing, jumping in pirouettes, twirling a flag, playing a flute or a clarinet, pulsing out a beat on a keyboard, and making so much racket that I couldn't hear my guitar until I was on stage.

"How are ya'll tonight?" I asked timidly into the microphone.

"Alright!" someone shouted. "Play us some music!"

I laughed. "I will. It's crazy backstage, so much I can't hear myself think, much less tune up my guitar, so just give me a minute and let me get it tuned here in the quiet." I quickly made a few adjustments, my hands trembling, but that helped me to calm myself before I started the song. "I bet most of ya'll grew up listening to Mother Maybelle." I heard some audience members, "Yeah! That's right!"

I smiled. "I did too," I said. "Even though I didn't have a Mama living, I'd listen to the Carter Family and imagine I was playing right along with them on 'Wildwood Flower', so here we go." And I jumped right in as if I had watched Mother Maybelle on the stage, and she taught me everything she knew. I'd been listening to that song since I was a baby, and I like to have blistered my fingers every week trying to pick it out on the guitar at Miss Emy's. The old folks tapped their feet and reflected the nostalgia of days gone by in their nods and joyful faces. I didn't miss a note and was so proud of myself after I finished that I knocked over the microphone stand while I was trying to say thank you and take a bow. Most of the audience stood and applauded, except for some of my school mates who sat in a back corner and giggled at my old timey country music.

"That's alright," the announcer said, "we'll pick it up. Thank you, Robin Ballard, for sharing your musical talent with us." Then, I nearly tripped on a cord stretched across the stage. "Two left feet," he said. "Folks, she just might be funny enough to be June Carter. It's all part of the act." It wasn't, but I was relieved that he made it seem that way.

By the time I got backstage and put my guitar in the case, I could hear Leslie Jenkins singing on stage. The a capella performance was perfect and filled the building. She did a variety of gospel songs that melted the hearts of everyone in the audience. She started light and easy, then brought out "Amazing Grace", and ended with a revival of "Swing Low, Sweet Chariot" that prompted the audience to join her in clapping the rhythm before giving her a standing ovation. The whole auditorium erupted in cheers and shouts, and "Praise Jesus!" She was overwhelmed when she returned backstage, tears streaming down her face. "I never tell anyone, but I am always terrified," she said to us, as we crowded around her to compliment, "Wow, your voice is beautiful," and "Congratulations. That was amazing."

After the talent portion finished, we put on our gowns again. Everyone was so consumed by the talent performance, they had forgotten about the judges' questions for the final round of the pageant. We lined up in two rows on the stage and stepped forward when it was our turn to answer.

The judges took turns asking questions. During a previous year, Aunt Melinda had been a judge, and I was wishing that she'd been chosen again that year. One outside judge was brought in every year, and this person was usually the guest judge for the baking contest, the poke sallet cook off, the rose competition, and the beauty pageant. My question came from the out-of-town guest judge who was a news broadcaster in Atlanta. She asked me how I would approach the problem of poverty if I could do something to help the poor. I responded, "The poor feel the same as the rich. When the rich are hungry, they eat. When the poor are hungry, they sometimes steal. When the rich need to pay a bill, they get out their checkbook. When the poor need to pay a bill, they go to the pawn shop. So, I think the poor need job training— vocations and skills. If we can provide some way for them to earn a decent living in a steady job, then many of the poor wouldn't be poor anymore." My voice became shaky in the middle and faltered for a moment, even cracked on the word "steal," and I cleared my throat, drew in a deep breath, and continued. I didn't know if I would get my voice back to normal without crying, but I kept those tears at bay. The judges looked serious even though some of them were young and connected to local families. They were expressionless, so I didn't know how my answer resonated with them. I couldn't even focus on what the other girls said, as I was so preoccupied with analyzing what I thought I said in my answer.

Aunt Melinda sneaked backstage while we waited for the judges to make their decision. She whispered, "Your little shaky voice just made it that much better. And your Carter Family performance was great. So authentic." She squeezed my hand. "I love you," she said and quickly turned to go back to her seat. All night, I had wondered if my Dad would show up. Depending on where I was standing on the stage, the glare from the spotlights wasn't in my eyes, and I could see into the audience. I found Aunt Carolyn and her family close to the front. They waved and smiled, gave me a thumbs up, and even my cousins seemed interested. I noticed that Aunt Melinda, Miss Emy, and some other relatives had a row in the middle.

While we waited backstage, I peeked out the side door. Dad wasn't there, not seated with my relatives, not standing in the back of the room or slumped against the back doors. I slipped out the door, stayed behind the curtains that covered the wall, and hurried out into the lobby, where they sold refreshments and were taking down all the booths from the festival. I peeked down the hallway to the bathrooms. People stared at me and smiled. A few nodded and said, "Good luck" and "You all did great." I didn't see my Dad anywhere, and I was just hoping that maybe he was out there, buying popcorn or using the bathroom—anything—I wanted him to be present even if he wasn't interested or didn't pay attention. I wouldn't cry, I told myself.

Some men and women, who had been milling around the lobby, opened the big back doors into the auditorium. I heard someone say, "Is she the one?" I turned to go back to the auditorium and sneak behind the curtains to join the other contestants backstage, and I could see that everyone in the audience was looking toward the lobby. The other contestants were already on the stage.

"Oh, no," I said to the people closest to me, "I guess I'm late." I suddenly felt stupid and inferior, especially when I noticed Leslie Madison glaring at me from the back row of the audience. They must have called the girls onto the stage just after I left.

A few men in the auditorium were shouting to me and motioning for me to hurry. I started to walk faster and tried to run in my heels but stopped when I stumbled a little.

"Sorry," I mouthed. "So sorry."

"You can't leave yet, little lady," the announcer said into the microphone as someone gave me a hand and helped to hoist me up onto the stage.

"I'm sorry," I said to the contestants, and my face flamed in embarrassment and I felt my knees buckle for a moment once I got into place at the end of the line.

"You see, now that all of our lovely contestants are here, let's applaud them all," the announcer said. When the audience stopped clapping and cheering, he said, "And, since we had a little delay, I'll get right to the point. Your second runner up is Jenny Parchman." She screamed and jumped up and down as if she had won Queen. "And we love your enthusiasm," the announcer said. Jenny's family stood and screamed just as she did. They hugged each other and the people seated next to them.

"Alright, we've got quite a crowd tonight," the announcer continued. "Your first runner up in this poke sallet pageant is Leslie Jenkins." The Jenkins family rang cow bells and blew whistles. Leslie smiled perfectly with her hands out to the sides of her red dress. Her shoulders relaxed like a flower opening, and she beamed a smile free of elation or emotion. All the contestants moved forward to hug Leslie after her tiara was placed on her head. We fumbled through kisses on her cheek and not bumping into one another to get back into place. I thought she would be the Queen and was surprised by her second place finish.

I couldn't imagine who would beat her and tried to maintain my confidence, even though I felt everyone staring at me, and I was humiliated for not being on stage at the end. I could see Miss Emy, and she had that look on her face, like I had blown it. Aunt Carolyn was hitting my oldest cousin on the arm so that she would behave. A few of my relatives looked down at the floor in disappointment. Even if I wasn't going to win, at least I could have followed the rules. I didn't want to be known as the girl who wasn't on the stage at the end. I heard the questions ringing in my ears: "What was she doing roaming around the lobby anyway?" "How did she get out there?" "Didn't Melinda just go back and see her?"

The Parchman and Jenkins families continued to cheer and shout. "So proud of you, Jenny!" her Dad bellowed.

"And now, the moment you've all been waiting for. She may like to roam, but she's wise beyond her years and shines like a golden sun. This year's Poke Sallet Queen is June Carter. Just kidding, it's Robin Ballard."

I stood in that frozen, hand-to-mouth, pageant cry while all the contestants hugged and kissed me, and the audience clapped and cheered. Last year's queen, who had been introduced during my quest to find my Dad, and whose presence I hadn't even noticed on the stage at the end, placed a towering, glittering crown on top of my head. They placed a dozen long stem red roses in my arms. She tried to get the sash over my crowned head, and then realized that she should have done that first. I handed the roses to another contestant and the crown back to last year's queen. I placed my own sash over my head, took back the crown and placed the combs attached to the bottom of the crown into my hair, and then, retrieved the roses. I thanked the other contestant and last year's queen.

"Your Poke Sallet Queen!" the announcer bellowed again. Aunt Melinda screamed, "Robin! That's our girl! Robin!" Miss Emy motioned for me to wave, and I realized that's what I should do. I walked down the stairs that the ushers had placed at the end of the stage. I walked down the center aisle of the auditorium, waving to everyone, to my family and relatives, the other contestants—the people of my town, and I was in disbelief that it was actually happening.

When I walked outside into the spring air that night, I smelled everything that brought me happiness—visions in my head: plates of boiled greens, smells of earth and cake (one of my favorite combinations), the lush late spring, the deepening to the edge of sweetness, just getting a hint of it in the lettuces, cabbages, and spinach. The clover was full of wide luck.

CHAPTER 5

ASSIGNMENT FIVE

My Dad, Daniel, 2000

Okay, so I was avoiding it again and again, and the professor called me out on it. She wrote, *There's more to this! GO FOR THE REAL!* on the parts of the assignments where I mentioned my Dad.

After the Poke Sallet Festival, Dad was gone for what seemed like months, maybe an entire season, and then he was back soon, looking thin and transparent, talking to Miss Emy in private. I took a lot of walks, and for once, I really wished that he was dead, that he'd just never come back after stealing from me again, but then I imagined that he'd be alone and screaming as he did when his supply ran out. We thought he'd tear the place apart or maybe claw off his face. It was excruciating, and I had to leave, to block it out. His calls played in my head—the screaming, ranting, cussing me out. Demanding money from Miss

Emy, he shouted through the speaker on the answering machine, that she owed him for all the work he did on the farm, for the money he imagined that she handed out to his sisters, especially Melinda, for imagined abuses and neglect, for pity that his wife died and he was so weak. He tried every plea and argument to get money, to get anything some days. Anything he could sell, pawn, or trade. I trembled when he banged on the doors, rattling the frames, thinking he would rip it from the hinges and crawl through the gaping space. He didn't. Somewhere in my heart, I sensed the shame that eventually settled into his soul. It turned him in another direction or reduced him to wailing and crying while clawing the ground. These moments were my trembling times. I searched my forging mind and heart for a variation in my pattern. He was alien to me, an animal crying out for sustenance in a howling tremor that always receded as Miss Emy and I abided in dread of where his potential abuse might eventually go. Miss Emy was more in fear than I, since my mind tried to reason that, as my Dad, he must have more affection for me than he shows. I just came back and told Miss Emy to call one of my aunts, preferably Melinda, to come and get me.

At first, all the beginning of my life, I thought that being pretty was my talent. I saw it as the talent every girl should aspire to have. I wanted to be pretty and smart, but pretty was more important to me than anything else. I wanted to be treated as a pretty person is treated so that I could marry myself away to an escape, but when I was treated as the pretty person, I was sorry to be the pretty one and wished to be smarter or simply fade away and into the group. The change happened after I won Poke Sallet Queen and was recognized for my intelligence first. For me, it was significant that the announcer mentioned wisdom as his first description of me. I felt more confident when I could praise my own motives—entering the pageant not to be the pretty one, but to use that to win the scholarship money. I needed the funds for school, and I allowed my appearance to help get me there, but not as I had in the past with boyfriends in high school. To lead as the smart one might be better, I thought in high school, often too late and already in a bad situation. A misconception for the guy. He always said, after we dated for a month, "You were different before."

And, after the festival win, I asked the next guy who said something like that to me, "You mean before I wanted to talk about myself and have a personality?"

"Yeah," he said, relieved, "can we not do that?" He laughed and reached for my waist, pulling me closer to him. "Pretty, pretty Robin," he said and whispered, "so pretty you never have to say a word."

"What does that mean?" I was repelled that he believed it was okay to say all of that to me. It was bad enough to actually think it was acceptable to have those thoughts about me, but to verbalize it! If this kept up, I wouldn't even get the honor of a Bo Diddly song or ring without an accidental pregnancy or complete complicity. It was no longer acceptable to hang on while he bragged to his friends and flirted with other girls in front of me at parties. I witnessed the scenario too often, falling for it a couple of times before recognizing the pattern I was allowing into my life.

He laughed and kissed me. "You know."

"I don't, and I don't want to," I said, standing to leave.

"I'm just joking with you anyway," he said. "Can't you have a sense of humor?" I had already picked up my keys and was opening the door. My wish to be accepted finally gave way to a real moment when I could notice the imbalance and act on it.

What caused me to give up on boyfriends were the thoughts that I understood would happen later, after you've settled in. How do you know that you did the right thing, just jumped right in and had a family, kept on having kids, struggled with career and family, food consumption, schedules, whether or not you even liked one another, debt, the merits of voting, how to park the car correctly so that everyone could maneuver in the drive, when to call, and how to say that it was okay, and the look from someone's eye when it wasn't? I could see all of that in every couple I knew, and I shuddered and ran out of it before the relationship lasted very long; and with every guy where there might be such an eventuality, I made good on all the methods of sabotage that I'd learned.

Aunt Melinda helped me to move into my own apartment, and she cried when it was time to leave me. How much I longed to feel that way, as if I had a real mother—someone who always welcomed me with open arms and who was sad when we were apart. Yes, Miss Emy had done that, but my Dad had been her main priority. She was his Mama, and I never forgot that her goals had everything to do with him and his sobriety and independence from drugs.

In my new apartment, I felt loved and free—a bliss I couldn't have known I was missing until I experienced it. I cuddled under the blanket on my thrift-store couch in my too-breezy apartment, and looked out across the creaky, hardwood floors, out the big windows and onto the tiny, sunlit lawn and, just beyond, I could see the street, Lealand, which led me to school and the restaurant where I worked. If it was quiet, I could hear the traffic on the interstate, but couldn't see it from the house. I didn't have a washer/dryer, but Aunt Melinda's was only a short drive away, and I made it home to see Miss Emy at least twice a month. Admittedly, I went home every week at first, worried about how she was doing out there by herself. I still tended her garden. I drove into the Co-Op to have the old truck and tractor serviced once a year. Parking Hoot's old red Ford pickup felt like paddling up in your canoe with your horse, spitting chaw, while all the other farmers pulled up in Mercedes or Bumblebee Dodge Rams to the Co-Op. The big red Ferguson tractor was the same. Hoot's old truck and tractor matched in their way of conjuring snuff-scented hay clover moments with their snorting, rattling, earth-churning motion. Then, Miss Emy could run things just fine—do the trimming, mowing, and hauling— she just didn't like to drive on the highway to the Co-Op since it became so busy with the city connector.

Returning home every week didn't last long—the comfort of my own place and my own routine in the city soon settled in. The apartment was a small room with a kitchenette and a stand-up shower in the bathroom in a house built in the early 1900s. The house was split into three sections, and I thought I was the only tenant for the first year, since the others were so quiet.

My telephone kept buzzing. Aunt Melinda. I couldn't call her an annoying mosquito, since that would just be selfish and bratty. She was the most like a mother. Yep, mother bear. She starts asking, "What did you learn at school today?" Calling almost every other day to check in and ask about grades and classes, money, gas, if I'd been to the grocery. "No creeps lurking anywhere?" she'd ask like, "you just let me know, and I'll take care of 'em." Like a different, cool aunt. "You carrying that mace I gave you?"

When I visited Aunt Cora during this time to hear her stories, Aunt Melinda would cook a meal and insist that we eat together if it was during dinner time. She was shoving broccoli and chicken noodle soup down my throat, sandwiches and fruit in my pockets to take back to my apartment. I joked as she dished up a new, healthy meal that she'd learned to cook—lentils and stir-fried vegetables. Oh, how I missed the days of funnel cakes, ice cream, seltzer, and fried chicken. She left groceries on my porch in the shade and texted me about them. During the weeks when she was especially clingy, I pretended to leave my phone on campus or in the car. I was trying to finally escape the sensation that someone might barge in and take over my space. That's what always happened at Miss Emy's.

In my new place, I escaped to the silence. I sat in the courtyard out back and played the guitar, tried to make up songs and sing into the trees. The privacy fence made me feel like I was singing for the leaves and clouds and stars in the sky and the moon and my empty house until I heard applause late one afternoon. I shrieked in fear and fell backward when I saw the man standing in the doorway.

"I'm so sorry," he said and nervously adjusted his ball cap. "That was a beautiful song," he continued nervously. "Did you write it?"

I didn't answer.

"I'm helping my friend, Angie, move in some of her things. She's renting the apartment upstairs. I'm Kevin. I'm sorry for being a dumbass and scaring you."

"Oh, it's okay," I said. "I'm not used to seeing anyone. The place has been empty for awhile. I'm Robin."

"Are you in a band?"

I laughed. "Oh, no, just messing around," I said.

"Would you want to play in a band?"

"Yeah, right," I laughed.

"I'm asking 'cause we have a band—my friends, and I need a singer. Playing the guitar is a bonus."

"What kind of band?"

"We play what I just heard you playing. Folk, a little bluegrass, a little funky sometimes, a little twang other times." I didn't know what to say, as I'd never been asked to be in a band. Did I audition? Did they play gigs somewhere? Did they have an album?

"Yeah," he said during the awkward pause. "Well, I play the fiddle, as does my friend Angie," he pointed to the upstairs of the house. "And, Martin, our other friend, plays the standup bass, so we really need a singer and guitar player."

"What's the name of your band?"

"We just started, so we don't have one yet."

"Oh."

"Kevin!" we heard a voice shout from inside the house. "Help!"

He turned quickly to help his friend when we heard her shout again, "Never mind! I got it!"

"Yeah." He shrugged his shoulder. "I better go help out. She's a good friend, not my girlfriend." He blushed and tried to quickly say something else so that it wasn't obvious that he was dropping a hint to me. "Anyway, Martin has a little studio space in his apartment and we're planning to practice for the second time tonight, after we do a few things here. If you want to check it out, or just play a few songs, whatever, come over if you want. He lives over in The Village Square by the university, apartment 714. We'll meet up at 8, just come over."

"Okay," I said. "Thanks."

"Nice to meet you, Robin," he said. "Hope to see you later." He stumbled when he went through the doorway, back into the house.

"Did you meet one of the neighbors?" I heard his friend, Angie, ask him. The door shut, so I never heard the answer.

I met the whole band later that evening and played music with a group of peers for the first time in my life, and I was addicted from that night. Both Martin and I were students at the university, while Angie worked two jobs— one at a clothing boutique and the other at a restaurant— both located in the village, and Kevin was a nurse at the hospital. Even though he looked like a student himself, Kevin was four years older and in his first nursing job, but he always dreamed of having a band and playing in Nashville. After two failed attempts during college, he had given up on it until meeting Martin at the coffee shop. They seemed to have the same schedule and ran into each other there for months, and over the conversations, learned that both had the same taste in music and wanted to form a band.

Martin was studying music and recording technology, and already writing music with his friend Angie. He knew her from high school, but she hated classes and grades and swore that she would never attend another class after graduation. She had short, maroon-dyed hair that swirled around her face in little curls that she pointed in precise directions beside her temples and along the forehead. Some of them spiraled perfectly, giving her an otherworldly aura of floating and drifting, when surveyed with her thin, graceful frame. She placed three cups of coffee on the table for us. "Ballerina trained for fifteen years," she said dully after I complimented her posture and ease of movement, while we all sat around the picnic table outside the coffee shop and watched the people pass by— students crossing over to campus, bicyclers hurrying across the intersection's big curve and hopping the sidewalk, professors carrying paper sacks of groceries from the organic market across the street, drivers fighting over the parallel parking spaces, and all of the movers and shakers of the day in motion. Angie sat across from me, happy to be finished with work for the day.

"What's something about you that would surprise us?" Angie asked me suddenly, during the quiet space when we were all sipping our drinks and staring at the life happening around us.

I thought first about my Dad being homeless, but I couldn't tell them yet. I had only talked to my Dad briefly on the phone. He was out of rehab, had a sponsor, and was going to AA meetings almost every day. He was working again, selling *The Patron*, and I didn't want to imagine them looking for him on the streets around town. I hoped that my Dad would go in the right direction. When we talked on the phone, he had told me that he was trying to get into a communal house with some other men. Dad said, "They are real good about cooking meals and washing up after themselves." The house was affiliated with one of the shelters where he stayed, but I didn't know if he ever got into the house or not. I never called him back, falling into doubt and placing my confidence in his abilities to mess up and fail. I assumed that he would move again, running, more than likely, for failing to meet with his probation officer, but he assured me that he stayed clean, kept going to AA meetings, and rode a bicycle everywhere. There are always drifters around the coffee shop and downtown close to the university, but not in the village as much. They stayed closer to the shelter, closer to 8th avenue, the bus station, the venues for shows and tourist destinations, where they could get some change. I gave them my change. Couldn't refuse when someone asked, even when they were rude. I know they sleep on the sidewalk sometimes, and they think they deserve it. Maybe some think they deserve a palace bed and believe the concrete is marble—madness. Others do it just to be alone (as strange as it seems), but at least they aren't in a shelter crowded by all the other sleeping people, worrying about the shelter not policing those who would do harm. Maybe they needed to escape the madness of other people and have no place to go. I understood their fears and shame. Shame of stench and grime. Peril of being out there for too long. Ravaged by the emptiness of others and self. I saw loneliness control until ailments and illness forced them into an ambulance, and then a mental hospital for some, maybe jail for a couple, and anonymity for most until being released back into the parking area right there in front of the hospital or jail, and walking back into the death trap of not knowing where to go, but understanding the long walk it will take and the asking and begging along the way. The strife of regaining lost ground plagues most people like my Dad, but he had the gift of Miss Emy when he was willing to try. I focused on looking ahead, in a new direction that moved me up in life, and away from that pattern in my family. I didn't want to tell the whole story to Angie, Kevin, and Martin, and wonder about their judgments or if they would feel sorry for me or if I was too angry. My diatribe would make me seem like an insensitive ass unless I explained all the bad times with him and then I would feel protective of him if they condemned him—the double edged sword of truth. I sat in stunned silence.

"There has to be something funny you can tell us," Kevin said nonchalantly. Maybe he sensed my fear of a big confession.

"Oh! I was the Poke Sallet Queen," I said. Angie laughed, spraying her coffee into the grass.

"There you go," Kevin said with a big grin on his face.

"The what what?" Martin asked. "Like Elvis Presley? Poke Salad?"

"That's the name of his song, but the plant is called Poke Sallet," I said. "They have a festival every year in the town where I'm from and there's a pageant for a queen."

"The Poke Sallet Queen!" Kevin announced.

"Wow," Martin said shaking his head. "Well, do people really eat it, poke salad, or whatever it's called?"

"Yeah," I said. "Parts of the plant. They cook it in different ways. My family has always grown it—even in our medicine wheel."

"What's a medicine wheel?" Kevin asked.

"Um, it's a garden," I said, and found myself describing it for the first time to my friends. "It's shaped like a circle, and it's planted so that certain herbs are in their own section depending on what they treat or heal or are used for in cooking or teas. Something like that." For a second, I wondered if they would think I, and my family, were crazy, but their reactions were what I needed.

"That's so weird," Martin said, combing his wavy, auburn hair through his fingers and reclining on his other arm. "I like you more."

"Even more strange is that my family thinks there's gold coins buried out there from forever ago." I laughed.

"Amazing," Angie said. "How big is a medicine wheel?"

"Pretty big," I said.

"A buried treasure, too!" Martin exclaimed. His eyes lit up wildly. "Do you have a map?"

"I would love to see that medicine wheel," Kevin said. "Poke sallet in the family medicine wheel." He started singing the line like a bluegrass song. "Poke sallet queen in the family medicine wheel. Bring your pains and woes, tell her how you feel. How you Feeeeeeel! In the moonlight, follow the glow" (tap,tap,tap) "to the wheeeeeel, and she will give you the remedy to heal."

"That's really good," Angie said. "I know you're just playing around, but I'm recording it on my phone so we can do something with it."

Martin looked at me, "Seriously, a map?" he asked raising his eyebrows.

"No map," I said. "But, I did buy a metal detector and plan to go out there and try to find it."

"You two, this song is the treasure," Angie said, hitting my arm. "Listen to what Kevin just started."

"What other secrets you got that we can use?" Kevin asked.

That's when I knew that I needed to find my Dad, once and for all.

****

It had been a while, so I called him, and he asked if I would meet him somewhere. Talking to my Dad was never easy unless he wanted it to be, but it was time and I finally wanted to get something on paper about him. We met downtown at Riverfront Park. I didn't know if he was homeless or not when he suggested we meet there, and I didn't want to ask him yet.

My heart thumped in my chest with fear. I felt like I dragged my feet along the sidewalk to meet, like I had always trudged through his garbage to the next stage in life. He never gave me his time, unless he needed help with something, and that was giving away *my* time and energy again. That day, I expected a request from him or that he wanted to complain about something or someone. He was already there, pedaling a bike around in circles. "You like my wheels?" he asked. He had a Nashville Sounds baseball cap on his head, and his face was tan. He looked lean, as always, but healthy, even handsome. He hugged me for a long time. "You want to walk a little?" he asked, and I nodded. He pushed his bike along as we walked up the narrow park along First Avenue, slowly, up the hill toward Fort Nashborough. I was again shocked by him when he said, "I'm getting an award at the shelter."

My Dad was accepting an award; I puzzled over this idea. Of all the things on the planet! An award. I stopped walking and stood in front of him. "Really?" It was for his recovery efforts, his ability to help others and mentor them. He was doing all kinds of odd jobs, cleaning and stocking, and still selling *The Patron*, too. Could this be my Dad—smiling, standing solidly, and looking into my eyes? His eyes looked just like my own. The dark brown was rich as the tilled earth. The same depth reflected, but for different reasons. He said, "I'm inviting Miss Emy to be my guest at the banquet." He cleared his throat a few times, trying to get it out, as if it finally occurred to him that he had completely overlooked me and needed to justify why Miss Emy deserved to go. "She deserves to be there, for all she's put up with from me these years. I feel like it's the right thing to do by her." When he finally had something to celebrate, I wasn't the first person he thought about including and that stung me again.

I tuned him out by then. I fought back my tears and said the right thing because I did want to be happy for him. I wanted him to be clean and hold down a job and a place to live. "It's great for you, Dad," I said. "Miss Emy will enjoy it and be proud." To do right by both of them, I had to hide my own feelings again and deal with another letdown for me, even though I knew that Miss Emy had made sacrifices for both of us.

"The thing is—this award is probably getting me a job, and I want my Mama to know that I can change," he said.

Having heard the same line at a rehab and in Miss Emy's living room a few times over the years, I wasn't easily persuaded and decided to tell him about my life, even if he was too preoccupied with his own. "Sure, it'll be great, Dad. I'm happy for you," I said. "I like college," I continued, changing the subject. "I've been in a writing class, and I've interviewed Miss Emy and Aunt Cora and a lot of people in the family."

"What are you writing about?" he asked.

"Old family stories," I said, as we passed the rustic old fort littered with the trash leftover from a concert the previous night.

"Some good ones," he said, and I thought we would probably say our goodbyes soon. By then, he was looking around more than making eye contact with me. The sun began to heat up by the river and make it steamy.

"Yeah, I love hearing about Hoot and Zona," I said. "I wish that I could find Hoot's old journals though. Everybody says he wrote every day."

"Yeah, he did," Dad said. "I might be able to help you find his old books. Miss Emy told me that you've been looking for them." We turned across the street and headed toward the Capitol building.

"You know where they are?"

"I'm ashamed that I do," he said, taking a deep breath, and suggesting that we sit down on a bench. He propped up his bike next to us and scooted the backpack he had been carrying underneath his feet. "Hoot's books and a bunch of papers were in an antique trunk that belonged to Ma Zona, and I took it back when I was in a bad way. I sold the trunk and some other antiques I found in that bedroom upstairs where Miss Emy piles everything up. I needed the money to pay off a dealer. I'm sorry, Robin," Dad said. "I sold part of it to one of our cousins and another part to an antique store in Carthage that's gone out of business since then." He put his hand on my jumpy knee. "I'm real sorry," he said, his voice shaking. He was going to say more to me, but someone he knew from the shelter interrupted us.

"Hey, Daniel, my man," the other man said. "Jim told me about somebody needing help down here with window washing, but I can't find the businesses he talking about."

"What's it called?" my Dad asked.

"Arcade," he said, and I could smell the cigarette smoke that clung to his dusty clothes. I worried that his scent would be worse if he came any closer to us. These thoughts were always a burden, but a truth of the human condition.

"You came too far. You need to turn around, go back about three blocks diagonal, that way," my Dad pointed. "It's real big. You'll see it. There's a big sign in the middle of it. A big U-shaped building."

"You want to come with me?" the man asked. "They paying cash. Wash windows." The man shrugged and smiled at me.

"I gotta finish talking here first," Dad said. "I'll meet you over there."

I was ready to say our goodbyes anyway, so that I could hide the shame I felt for having anger and disappointment at a time when he was doing better.

"You need me to walk you back to your car or something?" he asked.

"I didn't bring my car," I said. "I walked."

"From 21st?" he asked, as if he were surprised by the distance I covered on foot.

"It's not that far," I said. "I'm meeting my friends somewhere else anyway. I don't have to go all the way back on foot."

He hugged me and kissed the top of my head. "I'm proud of you," he said, putting the backpack over his shoulders.

"Thanks," I said. "I like your bike," I said, as he picked up the handlebars. He smiled, and we waved at the same time as we turned in opposite directions to leave.

I was grateful that he gave me a new clue and a new direction about where the missing journals might be, which made me closer to solving all of the family secrets. I decided to run an advertisement in the Granville daily newspaper. I gave a description of what I was looking for, where the journals were last seen, and my contact information. I wanted the other parts of the stories.

CHAPTER 6

ASSIGNMENT SIX

Aunt Cora, Revisited

I never liked to redo something if I messed it up, but I would get it perfect even if it meant redoing it over and over again. I began to approach my life as if I were learning a new song on the guitar. Our professor told us, "Assignment six is about revision. I want you to go back to one of the earlier assignments and revise it. Make substantial changes."

I didn't want to do that on my own and decided to ask Aunt Cora extra questions to make my revisions easier by giving me more information. Adding to something was a much more appealing task to me than refining, but I would do both after visiting Aunt Cora.

"Why did they keep planting the medicine wheel?" I asked her.

"Healing," she said. "The symbol of the family to keep going, the circle of the sun, the cycles of the moon, the food for hungry mouths, the meeting place to think it all over. Mama always said it would hold us together. The medicine wheel would protect us and the land, but I don't think it did. She wanted that kind of magic to work."

"What kind of magic? What do you mean?" I asked hesitantly.

"Unbreakable family bonds," Cora said. "That's what she wanted, really. But you can't just have your own way to have unbreakable bonds. It's a trick. You've got to give some space to those bonds before they can get strong enough to be unbroken."

"You think your family's bond was weak?" I asked, taken aback by her assessment. "Most of my friends don't know anything about their extended families, and never even knew their great aunts."

"You start telling a story and you have to tell it out," Cora said. "Sometimes, one telling is enough and it gets all quiet and low and something is healed, and it's never spoken again. But other times, one telling is not enough because it keeps getting told by different tellers and goes on its own telling and retelling, and gets beyond what it was. Becomes like a myth or maybe something worse— like a cursed spell—is what it feels like when it's your own life.

"Even different from all of that are the little stories, the ones we tell over and over to write our own versions of the truth," Cora said. "Those are funny. I used to get so sick of Jane's version of my life. Hearing someone else's take on it again and again. Wishing they would tell it correctly, but being downright intimidated by their ability to talk, to tell it so that everybody is captivated." She leaned back and smiled toward the distance, the blank screen of the wall. "Yes, she could spin a yarn. Jane. But she was loyal to me. No, wouldn't ever tell anything I told her not to tell. She kept my confidence to the death. Bless my sister." She turned to the empty chair.

"Robin?" She looked toward the hallway. "She must've left," she muttered.

"Over here," I said from the other side of the room.

"Well, you got so quiet I thought you'd already left." She laughed. "It's awful hard to be the only one still living," Aunt Cora said. "They've all died and left me here." She stared at the far wall for a while, and then blinked at me quickly. "You look like Paul, and he was my baby, my only baby. Mama just wouldn't let me tell it and nobody knew it either. Nobody knows it. You don't know that you're looking into the face of your great-grandma. You just know me as Aunt Cora." She pointed her knobby, arthritic finger at her own face. My mouth fell open upon hearing confirmation. I was not expecting her to say that— to throw those words out like they were a charge, an accusation, like they were scripted for the stage.

She reclined in her chair and just continued with the story, "First, I had the kitchen outside in that house that became your Daddy's and burned down. Mama took forever adding the kitchen to the house, and I don't think she ever would have if Ben hadn't made her. Ben was the oldest of us. Thirteen total, but Mama only birthed twelve—even though she claimed my baby for her own, he wasn't hers to take. I wished I had known that having a baby isn't about shame, even if the mother is alone, but times were different then. Nobody ever visited, and I guess I was too old to continue living without being with a man. I didn't know what to do once I was with a man. I just wonder how Mama could be cruel enough to keep me in the dark. Jane tried to tell me, but she married so quick that she didn't stay home for long at all. She used to joke and say, 'I can see it in Mama's eyes. She'd keep me back here on this farm forever if she could. With her and Nenny until I was buried a way back yonder on the Fulton Hill with the family.' In hindsight, Jane wasn't kidding me because that's exactly what Mama tried to do to me.

"Mama was already old, so I don't know how anybody believed that she had Paul at forty-eight-years old. I guess it was on account of her always looking so young and being a midwife, and then her reputation.

"If Paul had a normal family, maybe he wouldn't have messed up his life later. But, he never met his Daddy. Never saw Harold again, and Paul was so young, too young, when he found out that I was his Mama. What he did to his life after that! Child, I can't help blaming myself. I knew he drank too much, and I think it did kill him, caused that stroke after his hip replacement, and that was it. I'm just glad he didn't suffer, but I wish he could have seen all his grandbabies, especially you, Robin. You're a throwback to him. Nobody would've believed it on account of your Mama being so fair, but when you were born, you were almost brown as a chestnut. Still are just perfect, so pretty. I can see Harold in you. As I get older, I always wish that my younguns, my child's children and their little children will have some happiness in life. That you'll be able to love your babies, and not drive yourselves to being drunkards, and all that craziness out there.

"Paul just couldn't be satisfied, and I think it's 'cause of me, on account of my being his Mama and keeping it a secret, and when I told him about that rumor being true, when Dr. Davis's son said it was, I think he done the unthinkable. That's why nobody never seen that boy, Dr. Davis's son, again. I think he made that boy disappear so he wouldn't hurt me and Paul. But, I can't think on it too much cause it makes me feel low, and I'm trying to stay as sharp as I can."

She looked up at me and stared into my eyes, "Robin, you need to know the truth, and I might as well make the most of the time I got here. Nobody can't roll over and wish to be dead without just a-laying there and being nothing. Now, that ain't me. I got to remember what today is, and that's the last time I want to tell the true story, you understand?" I nodded my head. "Here, take this," she commanded me and held up a small wooden box.

"Open it," she said, shaking it a little to suggest I should move more quickly to take the box.

I was speechless, afraid to change my facial expression from the welcoming, bright look I had maintained during her shocking revelations. I was uncertain about whether I should embrace her as "Grandma" with a hug, or act as if she'd never told me anything. I grabbed the box and opened it.

"That's my wedding ring. Dalton, my sweetheart, the best man in my life, he bought it at a special jewelry company in Nashville. He treated me the way Harold should have treated me. He gave me everything, but I couldn't have any children for us."

The box was lined with a thick salmon-colored cushion for the ring, and the back of the box was smooth, creamy silk with the words B.H. Stief Jewelry Company 404 Union Street Nashville. The ring was carved and covered in diamond chips, sparkling in craftsmanship and detail. I was mesmerized by the simplicity and the intricacy at the same time.

"The way I always told the story," she continued. "I might as well tell it again. I had it memorized. I had to on account of Mama and Dr. Davis."

She changed her tone and almost the accent of her voice when she told her lie again—the way Zona instructed her to practice by heart:

"Everybody was out in the back, back field, a way back yonder working that day, out on the Fulton Hill side, and I was the only one at the house. Mama went out with them, but she come back about 3 o'clock, and I was making side pies, and already had the dinner ready 'cause I knew they'd be hungry, all them boys and men, that evening. Mama said she was pretty sure the baby was gonna come real soon. And round about 5 o'clock, it did. She was a-huffing and carrying on, pacing the floors and around the house, and then she went in her and Daddy's room. She just squatted right over the chamber pot and birthed him in about 20 minutes. But the afterbirth wouldn't come, and we were waiting and waiting. She started to cramp and cry, and the baby, Paul, he was just fine, so pretty, the prettiest baby there ever was. I put the blanket in the drawer by the fireplace after she put him to her breast for a while. And still, the afterbirth wouldn't come, and it was starting to get dark by then, 'cause it was just first of April. None of them boys had come back yet. We didn't know that a cow was stuck in a mud hole and they were delayed. So, we had to send for Dr. Davis, and he got the afterbirth and left and about that time all those boys showed up.

"And, that's how I told it, over and over, by heart. And, it broke my heart every time, but I learned to go on with things. Problem was that Dr. Davis told his son, and maybe his son remembered seeing Zona, instead of me, come for the doctor.

"It took so many years, we thought everybody had forgotten it. Then, Dr. Davis's son came home from school and got to drinking with Paul. He just told it out like Paul should've known it. Well, here comes Paul asking me what this Davis boy was talking about. I knew Paul could see it in my eyes. I told him the same story that I told everybody else, but he knew in my eyes that I was his Mama. I didn't have to tell him those words. He knew how Mama done me wrong and kept me there to raise him, and it all made sense to him, how much Mama was always on me to tend to him, unlike anyone else, how she always held me responsible for his behavior, and how she wouldn't allow me to leave, to have a boyfriend or get married, to go anywhere. She run off all my courters 'til Paul was almost grown. I married Dalton when Paul finally turned 18, and I'd been courting with Dalton for about three years. He was the sweetest man, and he loved me even though he knew I could never have babies for us. He saw how much pain I had every month, hemorrhaging and cramping up, until they had to take it all—my uterus and all—two years after we were married."

I sniffled and wiped away my tears. "Honey," she said, "Mama was fierce."

Cora described to me how she tucked the baby against herself, in the curve of her arm, sacred space next to her heart. *My baby*, she thought, and felt calm, as if there were nothing else in the world to matter, and no one else to care about. Just those soft hands, pink pads on the fingertips, folds in his legs like someone had tied pieces of string around him to create the fat rolls. She listened to Paul's breathing, the warmth and softness and his big eyes turning to look into hers with trust and innocence. The faster way his breath would pant when he wanted to nurse because he was hungry, because he was sleepy. His eyelids drooping over his dark eyes. He pulled against her breasts, squeezing the nipple between his gums and pulling again, making her breasts sink and swell with more milk. The breast deflated as he drank and gulped, then he stopped, catching his breath, looking up toward her, smiling momentarily, then grasping her breast again and drinking more milk. He rubbed his feet together as he drank, the tiny toenails scratching against the bottoms of his feet. He became more and more relaxed. He breathed and drank without having to pause or without becoming choked up. She liked the way that his tiny body stretched in abandon in her arms, his hand thrown out over his head. She could place him in the dresser drawer and get some work done.

Sometimes, when she got to thinking about why Harold left and how her Mama claimed the baby as her own, Cora felt the tears pierce deep into her breasts and she wanted to grab Paul and run, at least out to that cabin in the woods where Jane used to sneak off to. She wanted to be safe and open. Zona never had anything to do with the baby anyway, and Cora couldn't believe everyone was tricked so easily. Zona spun her mystery, her deliberate intrigue, focusing on others, complimenting their clothes or talents, deflecting any interest in the baby. Regardless, he wasn't anything special, only one more in a long line of boys. Everyone shrugged it off as Zona being old and getting surprised by another one, and Cora being old enough to want one for her own but being too awkward to get a man. She was always stuck out there on the farm, cooking and cleaning for all of them. Her extended family knew she was treated as the servant and Zona had made it that way, taking advantage of her naiveté. Cora caught on after the baby.... She then understood just how much she had given when Zona said the baby was hers, when he called Zona "Mama" and when she was forced to stop nursing by a mother who had learned to control Cora's body, too.

Cora sat on the side of the bed, preparing to nurse the baby. "If you nurse him too long, he'll know how to ask for it and then everyone will know what you and..." Zona said before she snatched up the baby Paul and left Cora sitting on the bed in the early morning light. Cora called down the hallway, "He has to eat! Bring him back to me!"

At the door, Zona turned, "I could just take him to town all day and then you'd have to wean him." She smirked.

"Please, Mama," Cora begged. "Bring him back." Cora's breasts swelled and ached, while Zona went out onto the porch with Paul crying back at Cora.

"Neh!" he called and stretched his head to watch Cora as long as possible. Cora's tears fogged her vision, and she banged her right breast into the doorknob.

She cried out, "Baby," and stumbled onto the porch. "Mama! Please!" She screamed and screamed when they weren't on the porch or anywhere in sight. She wailed into the foggy morning. "Mama!" and tore through the brambles looking for the way. Listening, she heard Paul crying. She ran, ran, clutching her breasts that had swollen with milk that dripped down the front of her shirt, saturating it to the waist. She breathed so heavily that she couldn't hear the baby anymore. She waited, trying to make her own heart be quiet. Oh, that heart wanted to fly up and look out like a hawk and swoop down on her Mama. It was too quiet while she waited, and her breasts throbbed all the way underneath her armpits and into her neck.

She heard the baby again and ran toward the hot spring. When she stumbled, she noticed Zona's shoe prints in the path. She ran as fast as her legs would go, certain that she would push her Mama and kill her for the baby. She feared the strength in her milk, warm and glowing with life, full of the stars. She yelled, "Mama! I will kill you!" She screamed something primal and terrible. She continued to run, prepared to fight. And then, she tried to stop because something was in the path. But, she jumped over the baby. She swirled around and looked at him, seated in the middle of the path, screaming, crying for his "Neh. Neh." His little tooth was bright in the sunlight, and his bronzed skin shone with furious sweat. She scooped him into her arms and gazed through the slits of her growling eyes, looking into the forest for Zona, but she was gone, leaving the chase, and abandoning her scheme for an unsuspecting day. This day was only a warning. A demand. Paul was already banging his head against her sternum. He looked up into her face and smiled for an instant, so happy to see her face, then screamed in hunger again.

"Alright. Alright," she said sweetly and looked into his face for a moment as she walked toward the rocky overhang next to the hot spring. The water vaporized and added to the dissipating fog. She shivered under her nightgown, but sat on the moist stone and winced as the baby sucked quickly from her swollen breast. She used his legs to rest her other breast and tucked him against her skin to keep his body warm. Leaning down to her forearm, she wiped the sweat and tears away from her face. She peeked into the coat and petted his hair and cheek. She kissed his face and his feet pushed into the folds of her stomach and back. He grunted and cooed as the hunger subsided. She broke his latch so that she could move him to the other breast, which was swollen and throbbing in pain, and he screamed out in anger and began to cry. He opened his mouth widely and sighed as he began to suck again.

"It's alright, baby," she said. "Neh Neh's here." He choked as the milk sprayed out of her nipple. She held him up quickly and patted his back. He looked at her and smiled and turned back to her breast to drink more. He gulped and gulped, his eyelashes fluttering with each big drink, and then he stopped and breathed. The milk sputtered in her breast, stopping its flow, descending into the ducts. He smiled and drank again until his eyes closed longer with each flutter and shut for a long drink. He pulled his ear forward and rubbed the hair tickling his neck.

What if her Mama tried to take him again? What if she left one day and went to town, as she had threatened to do, or went to visit her sister or cousin, and the baby was gone all day, or for two days? Zona could stay away a whole week, Cora realized. There was no use fighting it—

Cora could lose the *painful* way or she could begin weaning Paul with some of her own terms and without the fear of Zona running away with him.

Certainly, I didn't know what to say to Aunt Cora or to anyone else. Part of me wanted to run as fast as possible outside, call Aunt Melinda and tell her everything. "Aunt Cora is really your grandma!" I worried over whose number to dial first—Miss Emy's or Aunt Melinda's, and then it struck me that Miss Emy must already know. She keeps the secret. Maybe that's why I kept it for a while, too.

CHAPTER 7

ASSESSMENT AFTER THE ASSIGNMENTS:
Redemption

After the class finished, my newspaper ad paid off, and I got the journals—notes about the farm, another recipe for whiskey, the daily roundabout of life, some of Hoot's business accounts.

An old man had been waiting on me—that's what it felt like. Just waiting to hand the papers over to me with his shaky hands, but who knows what he was waiting for, but he had waited patiently and he didn't want anything for them. "Just use them wisely," Rex had said, as if it were some kind of prophesy, and I guess for my life, it was, and I needed to accept that. In his younger years, Rex was a tall, lanky redhead with freckles, but when I visited that day, his skin was ashen, and he was so thin that his bones looked like they would break through the flesh. He seemed to tower over me if he stood, and he was so weak that I thought he'd collapse from the effort. His daughter was in the kitchen and scolded him, "I told you to let me know if you needed something. There ain't any sense in you standing up. I'm making the coffee and I'll be in there in a minute."

"I need to stretch from time to time," Rex said. "It's good for me. I reckon I'm about as worn out as I'm going to get." He laughed in a chuckle. His eyes narrowed into watery slits when he thought something was funny.

His daughter brought coffee from the kitchen and sat on the sofa beside me. She had read the newspaper advertisement, told her Dad about it, and called me two weeks after it first ran in the paper. "I remember your Daddy coming here with that old furniture," she said. "I was about to run him off, 'cause we all knew he wanted money. He was begging everybody in the family then. None of us has seen him since, so I hope he's alright. I don't mean no disrespect to you, sweetie. That's just how it was."

"I understand," I said.

"Anyway, he had all that furniture from Miss Emy's house," she said. "We didn't know whether to call the police or what to do, but my Daddy told us to just hold on a minute and let him see what was there. He decided to take it all, called Miss Emy and told her it was all over here and she could come and get it all whenever she wanted, but she just hung up on him. Slammed the phone right down every time he called her. Isn't that what she done, Daddy?" she asked Rex.

"Yes, that's right," he said with an exasperated shrug, "I called her a half a dozen times, told her to send somebody for it, and every *time* she slammed down the phone."

"She didn't say anything?" I asked.

"Yes, the last time," Rex said. "I asked, 'Miss Emy, are you in your right mind? I've got your property and you keep hanging up on me.' She yelled into that phone, 'Rex Ballard, I'm sharp as a tack and I don't need your charity. Don't call me again.'" He laughed again. "That was that until your notice in the newspaper."

I stayed the whole day and listened to stories about his life. Rex was Hoot's younger second cousin, and he worked with Hoot, "got chased through the woods and along part of the ridge by the feds, but I got away, run clear on over to the knobs, I did," he said. "And stayed there, laying low for a while. Got chased a half dozen more times 'til they finally caught me. I served ten months." He laughed. "I was proud of that. Old Hoot, he never spent more than a few hours in the county jail. Some man done twenty years for Old Hoot, but he paid him well, I'll tell you. Hoot and the mob. It isn't nothing to talk about nowadays. Things ain't the same at all. It's all gone and they're all dead, I reckon. My old heart is just too amused to slow down, just keeps herself kicking. Your great-granddaddy was something else, and I had a time with him, had a time. Wonder what that old place is like over there now? My old place is done had it. I had to sell a big part of it, and they'll just sell this when I'm gone. The kids will. They got plenty of kids to take care of themselves, so I reckon they need the money. What about you? You all gonna keep Miss Emy's place?"

I shrugged. "I don't know. I guess that'll be my aunts' and my Dad's decision."

"I wouldn't play my hand based on guesses," he advised. "If you're the one interested in it, you should let her know. Don't lose your family's place. Nothing can replace it. Don't know what I'd do if I couldn't be here in my home—in my place when it's time for me to go. I've lived this long, and I wonder why some days, and maybe, part of it is to help you." He reached his hand toward me. I held onto it—the smooth, slippery skin wrinkled in rolling age spots and veins—and knew that we would never see each other again once I left that day. Rex died three weeks later.

Hoot, 1962

Still keeping the business going. Just got one man working for me, and just my old time locals and sometimes a young man will know a real drink and want one, even want to stock it. I got enough clients to keep me alive and capable of having a good time and a good Christmas. That's what I focus on…the moments with family.

Melinda is Paul and Emma's second daughter. She reminds me of my mother. Every time she visits, she grabs a little shovel and starts planting something. She doesn't want to wear shoes in the gardens, but we have to make her, and she ignores the horses. Jane and Cora tended the garden and snuck away to ride horses. Jane didn't want to plant a thing, never cared for the process of growth and transformation, until Cora cared and received attention. If we brought Cora the food, she'd cook a supper that caused everyone to nap, caused us to want to build a big fire or take a long walk. The swing on the porch was swaying through dusk and into a deep nighttime. Shivering in the dew. I miss the days of finding my children on the porch, hearing them up too late and too early. They have gone to make lives for themselves. I've been happy that Paul's family stayed here, and that he has an interest in farming.

Melinda can be a mess, poking and rooting through the wardrobes, the pictures, albums, and boxes. She likes to prowl. Her sister Carolyn is kind and agreeable. Even though she's the oldest, she will follow her sister. Zona scolds them and then starts teaching them some story. She makes up half of it. Least I think she does. I might just be fooling myself. I think that I probably have been since the beginning. I don't fully accept her spiritual reasoning. Just last week, I came upon them in the wheel, and Zona was seated among the tea herbs, holding Carolyn and Melinda's hands, and saying, 'We are thankful for the plants to heal us, to protect us, to help the babies be born from that other realm into ours, to be strong and wise, to be forthright and care for our elders, to be powerful women in the eyes of Creation. We ask for the Spirit!' She raised their hands in hers to the sky. While I have a tremendous respect for those of conviction, I'm what they call, practical. I'm amused and humbled by religion of any sort. Carolyn seems that way, but I think it affects her more than she reveals to me. She mutters while chopping at the earth with her shovel. She holds it over her head and pounds it into the ground. Dirt sprays their dresses as they plant, but they keep on digging as if their dresses were nothing. After the hole is deep enough, they drop in bulbs or the roots of new plants, whatever I've found for them to plant. They are proud of planting. The sweat makes their hair stick to their faces, and they have dirt rings under their necks. I would have lived forever as a pa and continued to have children, yet being a grandpa brings comfort in old age.

****

I kept reading and, not far into the first journal, there it was. Hoot suspected the secrets that Zona forced Cora to keep. I felt honored with a treasure but pulled by the pressure to tell it, and how, and who gets to know first and what should the delivery be like.

Hoot, 1968

Won't be long now, 'til I won't be talking anymore. Won't be writing a word. I'm going to hide these notes in the trunk and pray Zona doesn't open them. Maybe it would be best for her to know after I'm gone. That's what I consider some days, but other times I think it would be best to give them to Melinda, though she's a young girl yet, and I don't know that she should be reading a man's daily observances. There's nothing vulgar or incriminating in my writing. I have considerations and documentations. Confessions never appealed to me since I don't have any secrets. The biggest challenges are the years I struggled with the truth about Cora, and how I was a fool to Zona's deception. I had burned up inside when I realized it. Felt like the color red inside my heart. Like the pokeberry stain on those homesick letters that became my friends during those years. I learned what it meant to feel betrayed, as so many of those men wrote in their letters back home. They were heartbroken in many ways. I guess that any man who knows the betrayal of his country and then the way his wife could hurt his own daughter in such a cruel way, then it's a man who knows the turn of sickness from deceit.

I don't know why she did it, destroyed the letters between Cora and Harold, and kept Cora there. Took her only child. Shamed her.

I'm a person who is more humor than pain. I left punishment and failures to settle up with those city men, the big shots. I didn't bring violence to my hometown, and if somebody round Granville or the near counties didn't pay me, then he didn't get any more liquor. I didn't send my boys or my sons to hurt a man, even though they tell me that Ben did a lot of threatening, and my connections helped them to understand that he meant business if necessary.

Why do we destroy our words? Our letters? I kept those from the soldiers locked inside a box in a cabinet with a lock. Those men in the war, they saved a few berries frozen and thawed and used those to write a note, and another, and another, so the letters would keep arriving from a beloved, a wife, a mother. I didn't want Zona to rid us of all traces. She felt no sentimental attachment and would burn the belongings, the history. She didn't want to keep unnecessary items. I locked the guns, long rifles and all, in a case. The signatures engraved with the dates, 1815, 1825, 1869 and the towns, Roanoke, Haroldson City, Hickory. The rifles were crafted with engraved scrolls of flowers and vines, a snake, and intricate, geometric designs on the barrels. I took pictures of all of it, so I could keep a count on what I had. Children are also mischievous and if they get their eye on something interesting, it may end up with their belongings. I polished the silver in the drawers and dusted the wood, kept it free of cobwebs and debris so she had no reason to touch anything near my cases. I made a box for the arrowheads. We were both neat as pins and the children have learned the merits of orderliness as they've grown up.

I miss their laughter. Our Sunday family meetings with the music and smoking a hog for everyone to eat. Happiness on all our faces. Drums and banjos. That's what disappointed me when I heard about Harold. He was a fine farrier but he had an ear for music and I enjoyed his guitar playing more than most. I always hoped he did something with it and that's why he disappeared, but he stayed in the stables, so I've heard.

There was a conflict between Zona and Cora from the beginning. It was the most difficult and painful birth Zona ever had, and then Cora was into everything, curious and too whiny early on, but the boys told me about the day that Zona broke her spirit. Spanked her until she was sick and told her, "No more. You do what I say when I say it." She left her to cry alone, left her to wail for hours and sweat. Just a little baby, but nobody told me the truth about Zona's cruel streak and I never knew it. She could be moody when I was nearby, but that's all she showed to me. Cora learned to be quiet and she stayed shy, since Zona didn't teach her any other way to be. She learned fast how to cook and that's where she stayed. Zona had wanted to get back outside, where she was happiest, and she felt like a girl child kept her from returning to the fields and farm work until the girl was trained for the house.

Cora always had her feelings hurt, always sulking, and this caused Zona to react with more hostility to her. When I look back, I could see the bitterness at dinnertime, the narrowed eyes, but I was engaged with my business and thought it best to leave the women's issues to the women.

Cora and I have never talked about it, and I've decided that there's nothing productive and good about bringing it up after all these years. I don't think that my heart could take it if she decided it was time to hate us. Old Man Gibbs told me that his son quit speaking to him, and asked if Jane was still coming to see us. That was some years ago, and he died last year, Old Man Gibbs, but I said, "Hell yes, Old Man Gibbs, and I'd be down there to spank her rear end, and your boy's too, if she deserted me after all these years." I was joking, and didn't think Gibbs could be serious. I thought maybe his age was catching up to his memory and making him forget. I said, "They told me two weeks ago that they were headed over to your house directly after leaving here."

"Well, they didn't come here!" he shouted and slammed down the phone.

I called him the next day, but he said he didn't want to talk to me.

At the funeral, Jane told me that they did reconcile, Gibbs and his son, before the old man died, but I heard his aunt saying, "You ought to be ashamed of yourself for the way you treated your Daddy these last few years. Abandoned him when he's all alone."

Jane asked if I wanted to buy the Gibbs land before the man was even buried in the ground. I just shook my head and motioned for her to be quiet. "She must think I'm crazy," I said to Paul on the drive back to the farm. "But she's the one who's senile."

"Born that way," he said.

We had a good laugh about that. "Least I have one daughter with some sense and a good heart," I said.

"She's a real lady," Paul said.

Paul was already showing signs that he was messing with trouble. Nothing but trouble, since my youngest boy, Roy, returned from the war. He was doing those drugs he learned about during his war times, and all that I didn't want to know about, but Roy said life wasn't the same anymore. He tried to tell me about needing to escape, and even tried to get me to put that junk in my veins. I said, "Only spirits going in me is down my throat. And they taste delicious." Those boys laughed at that moment, but I warned all of them, "If I catch you doing what he's doing, 'cause he's playing with pure evil, then I'm cutting you off. I won't have a lying heap of junkies around here. Roy, you better carry your weight and keep it together. You hear me?" He nodded. "All of you hear me?" They nodded and I looked them in the eye, but I could see the curiosity in little Paul. That's how I taught them. "You don't talk it unless you can walk it. And boy, you better be able to do a whole hell of a lot more than that, too."

"Run," Paul joked.

"Don't you be running lest somebody's got a gun or an unfair advantage, if you're alone against a group, but otherwise, you best not let me catch you doing any big talking and then running away."

"Yes, sir," he said, his face turning red.

They learned fast that I might be in a business that some didn't look at favorably, but I meant to do things honorably and for them to do the same. Seems ironic to think about teaching them when Cora was being mistreated by Zona, and seems like Cora would've got fed up and said something by now, especially since Paul is grown and has children. That's why she wanted to see those children born when Miss Emy gave birth. She's always hidden behind Jane, especially since they both married and moved away from Granville. Not much has changed about them in many ways. Jane's just the same, nosy, busy bee, catches peoples' secrets and innermost thoughts and worries.

Cora always has a cake ready, and a different kind. She'll cook a whole meal and allow you to be satisfied and quiet. Build a fire, even when there's a draft during the spring and fall, complete disregard for if it's winter or not. Walnuts in her freezer all the time, shelled herself, and when I visit she always bakes my favorite, black walnut cake. On the farm, she never served one at dinner, but gave it to me later, to take away and share with whom I pleased in my meeting area. I made a warm drink with coffee and my special jar, and people loved that in the wintertime. It was worth the long ride out, worth the trouble of snow and ice on the bluffs and hills. Cora's cakes won prizes every year at the Poke Sallet Festival, at the fair, and the cakewalks. Her cakes would be gone in an instant, just as soon as the line could form. She always had a special ingredient that made her cake a little different. She knows real magic.

****

Redemption happens as a surprise when you're expecting remorse or shame as a matter of judgment, but you finally give in to forgiveness. Two months had passed since I met my Dad in Nashville, and after getting Hoot's journals back, I was angry that my Dad didn't care more about me and what was going on with my life. He didn't call to check on me, and I was more upset about his lack of interest in me, his only child. Why couldn't I have a Dad who was more like Hoot or Rex, who cared about their children.

That was it—I was going to track my Dad down and get some damn apologies out of him, once and for all. I didn't care about an award and his progress. I deserved to be his priority, and Miss Emy should have enough sense to teach him that, if he was too selfish or sick or dumb or whatever, to understand what most parents already give to their children. Even though confrontation was the motivation, my attitude for that direction quickly dissipated while I talked to him on the phone and he explained that he wasn't in Nashville anymore, but had moved to a nearby city to help with a movement to open a homeless shelter. Dad was living under a bridge in a tent community and asked if I would attend a fundraiser, a dinner and silent auction during the upcoming weekend.

"I'm sorry that I haven't been in touch," he said. "This came up so fast. I'm trying to help these people and make a difference."

"What are you talking about, Dad?" I asked. "No offense, but how do you have the resources to help these other people get off the street?"

"I know it's hard for you to believe. I met Glen, and about a year ago, he started this whole movement and opened Everyone's Kitchen, a food bank and pantry here in Springfield, and he asked me to come help him since I've had so much experience on the streets in different situations. I'm a people person, you know. I want to help people and this gives me a way to do it. I've been there, on the street, for years. Working with Glen and the people at Everyone's Kitchen has shown me what it means to help other people. And, the thing is we are making progress, even if it's slow."

"Progress to do what?" I asked.

"To open a shelter here in Springfield," he said.

"How did you even get there?" I asked. "Do you have your bike and your job anymore?"

"Glen asked me to move, and I did. Yes, I've still got my bike and ride it everywhere. I've got a place to stay with some other men when I'm not staying in the tent city to help those people. Glen hired me to work in the kitchen, so I've got a better job now."

"Are you the cook?" I asked.

"Sometimes, if I need to be," he said. "People donate a lot of the food. I just help out, overseeing, cleaning, talking to people, and now, I'm out on the street again, trying to get people to come in and eat something."

"They have that many homeless in Springfield?" I asked. "There's not a shelter at all? I don't get it. They just have a food kitchen to feed them, but nowhere to let them stay? They have to make them go back onto the streets?"

"That's exactly right. Oh, yeah, a lot of cities are like this one," he said. "Robin, it would be great to see you and have your support at the fundraiser. Plus, I want to show off my smart daughter to everybody even if I didn't have as much to do with it as Miss Emy and Melinda. They deserve the credit for picking up the pieces, and you deserve the most credit for just being born so smart." He was becoming a true diplomat. Levelheaded and loving, my heart lurched at that comment.

That weekend, I found myself at Everyone's Kitchen, meeting Glen and other people who liked my Dad. Everyone's Kitchen was open for lunch and dinner every day, and they could provide some items to the people who came in to eat a hot meal. The problem was that the zoning commission in the town kept refusing to rezone for a shelter in the area where Everyone's Kitchen was located, which was mainly industrial with a couple of odd factories, welding and supply stores, automotive and machine mechanics, an old 1970s era bowling alley, a veterinarian's office, and a 1980s era YMCA. The bus stops were located in the middle of the little strip.

I parallel parked along the street and followed the small crowd going toward a big sign painted in psychedelic colors and images. The sign said, Everyone's Kitchen. As I got closer, I noticed that the image formed a cornucopia with grains, fruits, vegetables, mushrooms, flowers, bees, honey. I heard drummers. The flash of glittering light from a bright hula hoop swirled into my vision. A couple of college girls rocked the hoops around their necks and arms, their ankles and waists. Children picked up hoops and tried to imitate the girls. A group of toddlers and elementary-aged kids drew chalk flowers along the sidewalk and into the parking area. Balloons were tied to homemade signs, and little booths overflowed with items for sale—beaded earrings, tie-dyed t-shirts, pottery cups, origami animals, freshly-squeezed lemonade, homemade ice cream, friendship bracelets—everything to benefit Everyone's Kitchen.

I hadn't expected such a festival atmosphere and was pleasantly surprised. I didn't see my Dad anywhere, but walked inside and looked around. His photo was on the bulletin board inside. He was standing in the middle of the street with some other people, holding signs that said, "Show You Care!" and "Help Us Rezone for a Shelter!" I was relieved to see proof that he was there and had been doing what he said. I had my doubts about the truth of his story and whether or not I would see him.

I turned around and saw him at the coffee booth. He looked like me. His hair was long, and he added some weight to his thin frame, though he was still lean. His shirt clung to his arms and abdomen enough to show me that he still didn't carry extra fat on his frame. His face looked fuller and easier than usual. The intensity was replaced with a more thoughtful relaxation across his brow. I felt more relief that he looked better than ever, but I shuddered in apprehension. As he slurped the hot coffee, he turned and noticed me just then. We smiled and waved simultaneously, and laughed. We met each other halfway. When I hugged him, I could feel that he was different, and I wanted to believe in peoples' ability to change over time—to become better people.

We talked for an hour while he showed me around Everyone's Kitchen.

"What have you been doing lately?" he asked.

"Focusing on school," I said, not really thinking about my answer.

"This is the kitchen, where all the magic happens, so we can feed these people," he said, standing in the center of a small room, engulfed by counter space, refrigerators, freezers, the sink space, cabinets, the stove tops, and industrial dishwasher. They were a hodgepodge of brands and represented a variety of storage options from different decades. "Most all of these appliances were donated from different organizations—even old schools and hospitals," he said. "Glen has been smart about reaching out to the community."

I met too many people, shaking hands and nodding along, feeling a greater devastation with each smile received from these people with no place to call home.

"This is impressive," I said to Dad.

"What about you?" he asked and winked. "Miss Emy told me that you've got a band, and even sang a few shows."

"I'd hardly call those shows," I said. "Just little coffee shop gigs and a couple of bars."

"She said you've been writing your own music," he said, while motioning for me to follow him outside.

"I'm trying," I said. "It's fun and a good change from school and work all the time."

"You still working in the library at the university?"

I nodded. "Still at it."

Dad was on a search for Glen, and finally, someone told us that he was at the tent city under the bridge. Close to the river, I followed my Dad along a path that went behind a gas station and down below the highway bridge that crossed the river. Tents lit up my view once my eyes adjusted to the shadows under the bridge, which rocked back and forth as vehicles passed overhead. A man sat down on the bank of the river, talking to a woman wrapped in a blanket and smoking a cigarette.

Dad whistled lightly, and the man looked up and tipped his hand toward us before helping the woman to her feet. She tossed the cigarette butt into a pile of rocks. They turned away from the water and climbed the rocks toward us to the tent area. I surveyed the community and the shared spaces they created—an area for laundry, where they boiled water in a big pot over a small fire, and the clothes dried on a clothesline made from rope strung along some spindly trees and bushes nearby. A few rods and reels rested on fold-out chairs—the fishing area. I doubted how effective the place would be in extreme weather conditions or if it became crowded or someone intruded upon the scene and created problems. As things were, the place was in order as much as a place can be along the riverside under a city bridge.

"Where does everyone use the bathroom?" I asked my Dad before they could hear me.

"They made some areas," he said.

"Like what?" I asked. "It can't be sanitary."

"Glen," my Dad said to the man when he reached us, "this is my daughter, Robin."

"Heard a lot about you. I'm Glen Jones," he said. His shaggy gray hair curled around the edges of his ball cap. It had the Everyone's Kitchen logo on the front of it, as did his shirt. He wore cargo pants and brown boots. With dimples, he had an infectious smile, and he was quite tall with a pot belly. "I've been grateful to have your Dad working with us for a few months now," he said. "I think we're about to accomplish our goals. He has helped us get out here in the tents, to the people, and talk them into putting the tent city away once we get the approval for the shelter. This is Jenna," he said, turning to the woman who had shed her blanket and left it in a nearby tent. He turned back to me, "This is Robin. I've heard she's a songwriter and has a band that we might like to hear sometime."

"What kind of band?" Jenna asked me. I blushed and realized that she was about my age. We shook hands, and her dark eyes darted away quickly. She wore jean shorts, a t-shirt with the Everyone's Kitchen logo, and a pair of gray Nike tennis shoes. Her brown hair was in dreadlocks.

"Americana," I said nervously. "Folk."

"What's your band called?" Glen asked.

"Poke Sallet Queen and the Family Medicine Wheel," I said.

Jenna laughed. "I love that name. Do you have an album?"

"Thanks," I said. "No, not yet. We're starting our first. It'll be called 'Ripe for the Pickin.'"

"I like that, too," she laughed.

"Do you live out here?" I asked her.

"For about two years now," she said. "Yep." Her dark eyes looked deeply into mine for a moment before she fumbled in the pockets of her shorts and pulled another cigarette out of the pack. "You got a light?" she asked my Dad. "I'm out."

"Keep it," he said, after holding out the lighter while she lit her cigarette. "Let's go over to the benefit," Dad said to them. "That homemade ice cream is delicious. Come on."

"How's the crowd growing since I left?" Glen asked.

"A lot of people showing up," Dad said. "You'll be happy."

We followed him along the path. "Thanks for inviting me, Dad." I said. He grabbed onto my hand, and we walked toward the music.

****

The metal detector kept reflecting the sunlight in the window of my apartment, so I decided that I might as well try to find something. I couldn't stop thinking about Nenny's story and the gold coins. Was it possible for Little Flowering Plant and Woods Runner to have been real? I wanted to have a look for buried treasure myself.

I drove out to the farm, thinking I would be attracted to a spot of earth as if I were dowsing with a willow wand. I paced along the river, sweeping the metal detector back and forth, up and down the banks in my rubber boots, searching, searching, sweating in those black boots, feet stinking, armpits reeking, spending all this time finding nothing but bottle caps and lighter tops and spoons and cans and lids of cans and what looked like pieces of old equipment. I wasn't even sure. I went back again and again, fell asleep in my old room, even missed band practice. Kevin and Martin left bitchy messages. I forgot to eat decent meals again and again. I heard Aunt Melinda in my head, but I even crossed over toward Fulton Hill...damn thing just starts beeping as soon as I find the next scrap of metal or prong, a hair barrette.... You just have to wonder where this stuff comes from in the middle of a field. But then, it is near the river that floods sometimes, and people must pass by time to time, even if it isn't the most well traveled part. I work up the property, sweeping that metal detector, bleeping as if it were cussing after a while. That's what it was like since I felt it myself. Thinking, *what in the hell am I doing out here, sweating, like to have gotten snake bit and sprayed by a skunk.* I was exasperated and pouring with sweat beyond belief when Miss Emy came charging across the field like a bull.

"You need to get out of there!" she yelled at the same time I heard the snorting. "What in the world you doing?" she screamed. "You better, run. Run! Robin, run!" She screamed with all her life, and terror flapped her whole, tiny body. The blue and white print dress waved like a bandana. I did think that she might burst a blood vessel in her face or put her eye out with that fan waving at the same time, or clutch her chest or enact some other extreme scene, since every cell in her being vibrated in extraordinary movement. All of that ran through my head when I heard the snorting, the blowing, and knew.... It *was* the bull!

I was running before the thought clicked because she scared me so and she was running for me with her tiny self. The bull was in motion with dust under his hooves, but only for a pace; then he turned in a circle. Just to warn me. I didn't ease up until I was almost at the fence. He snorted to be certain I wouldn't reconsider. His massive hulk surging, wiggling his face side to side. I scooted the metal detector under the gate and climbed over, pausing on the top to watch the bull scrape at the ground, prying up the grass and rich earth. He scraped and blew through his nose. He stared at me again, taking a step in my direction, and scraping the ground again.

"Would you get down?" Miss Emy asked in an exasperated question at first, and then she commanded. "Get down, I said." Her face was red and she flapped the fan, standing at the edge of the medicine wheel.

I dropped my leg over the side of the gate and nearly wilted onto the dirt turnaround that connected the field to the back driveway. I almost couldn't regain my legs. My clothes were soaked through with sweat as if I had jumped in the river.

I met Miss Emy in the medicine wheel and we were both too exhausted to speak. I dropped the metal detector down between my legs, beneath the bench. She couldn't even wave the fan, but set it in her lap while placing her hands on her knees and taking some deep breaths. "What are you trying to kill yourself for?" Miss Emy asked. "And don't say the gold." She gazed from the corner of her eye toward me. "Biggest bunch of malarkey the Ballard family ever conjured up, and I swear it's put the worst big dreams in their heads and filled them with the nonsense of finding treasure. Superstitions and lost treasures—they beat all I've ever heard tell of." She laughed. "But, Robin," she turned toward me and resumed fanning herself. "You've got to stop this mess. You're a smart woman now, and doing alright in school and playing your music with a band. It's a waste of your time to be out here every day, going to end up dead from a bull goring or a snake bite or something. Get the poison ivy or a heat rash. You need to focus on what you've got going for you."

"I know, Miss Emy," I said. "I got caught up in all those stories and trying to find some trace of Little Flowering Plant and Woods Runner. What if the gold is real? A treasure?"

"Oh, if that story is true at all, *you're* the trace of those characters. There ain't nothing you're going to find out here to prove a thing." She shook her head to match the fan. "Now, don't you think all those university professors and geologists researching the meteorite crater out there would have found something? They've been looking at that crater and the hills around it for decades and decades."

"From what I understand, they never looked over here because they were over past the Fulton side, looking at the cave and the point of impact," I said. "I thought maybe there was a chance on this side."

She reached for my hand and squeezed it. "The gold is your family and all these stories you've dug up," Miss Emy said. "You've been able to get to know your great-grandma. *That's* the treasure."

"I know it is," I said, "and I was thinking what if I could show her those coins after all this time…"

"I don't know how someone as intelligent as you are could believe any of this nonsense about a treasure," Miss Emy said, exasperated, and turned to watch the bull recede along the hillside toward the river.

"You don't have to insult me just because you don't see it the same way I do," I said, pulling my hand away from her.

"Well, I don't intend to end up with a heart attack from trying to rescue you from the bull or something else! I'm sick of worrying about you out here all day. Finally, I don't have to spend all my days worrying about your Daddy and whatever craziness he's gotten himself into, and I don't plan on starting some new crazy business worrying about you. I'm just sick of watching you waste your time!" she said, becoming enraged as she lectured. Miss Emy stood abruptly, as I scooted in the opposite direction, thinking she was going to come at me. She'd never directed animosity toward me before, so I was already crying. She picked up the metal detector suddenly and threw it, and the detector hit a patch of lamb's ear and bounced under the hydrangeas. Beeping. Beeping. Miss Emy shuddered. I stood and hugged her tightly, kissing her teary cheek. The metal detector continued to ring a high-pitched vibration.

CORA'S RECIPES

Cora gave me these recipes to share. The measurements given are the only way she knows to relate the recipes. This is her advice: "Experiment, but be wise. Don't use any part of a plant unless you know what it is and what it can do for you. And, certainly, don't use plant parts that can harm you. Use only what can heal you."

BOILED POKE GREENS

2-3 Sacks of young poke sallet leaves

Salt

Bacon cut into strips, cooked. Hog's jaw, uncooked.

Vinegar (optional)

Wash leaves thoroughly. In a large pot, bring to boil enough hot, salted water to cover the poke sallet leaves. Boil leaves in water for twenty minutes with the hog's jaw. Drain and rinse the leaves. Repeat boiling the leaves, draining, and rinsing two more times. Throw away the hog's jaw. In iron skillet, fry bacon strips. Add boiled poke sallet greens and mix well over heat for two minutes. Serve similar to other greens—turnip, mustard, etc. Vinegar is optional. Cora served her poke sallet greens with sliced, boiled egg, mashed potatoes, and poke sallet corn cakes.

FRIED POKE SHOOTS

Sliced pokeweed shoots—a bunch

Egg

4 tablespoons flour & 4 tablespoons cornmeal

Salt & pepper

When you gather your poke sallet greens, keep the shoots (also known as the young stems), or collect before they are leafy and more like asparagus. Slice them like celery or leave them long like asparagus. Heat 2 tablespoons of oil in an iron skillet or use bacon drippings. Whisk one egg with salt and pepper in a bowl. Mix flour and cornmeal together in a bowl. Place slices of poke shoots into egg mixture, and then coat them with flour/cornmeal mixture. Fry in iron skillet until golden. About 2 minutes. Place on paper towel to drain excess oil. Serve hot. Taste great dipped in horseradish-mustard.

POKE SALLET CORN CAKES

1 1/3 cup cornmeal

1/3 cup flour

2 teaspoons of sugar

2 eggs beaten

2 ½ cups milk

¼ cup softened butter or oil

¼ cup minced yellow onion or thinly sliced green onion

1 garlic clove, minced

¼ cup prepared poke sallet greens according to the previous recipe

Combine all ingredients, mixing well. Drop batter by two tablespoons full at a time onto hot, lightly greased iron skillet or griddle. Turn cakes when they begin to bubble on top and edges look brown. Eat while hot and enjoy. Delicious with catfish.

ABOUT THE AUTHOR

Shana Thornton is the owner of Thorncraft Publishing, an independent publisher of literary and historical fiction. Her first novel, *Multiple Exposure* (2012), focuses on the impact of war on the family. She publishes the work of Tennessee author and attorney Beverly Fisher (*Grace Among the Leavings*, 2013) and Massachusetts author Melissa Corliss DeLorenzo (*The Mosquito Hours*, 2014, and *Talking Underwater*, 2015). Shana earned an M.A. in English from Austin Peay State University. She lives in Tennessee with her family.